Rhoda Rage

and the Goldfish Letter

A Mystery By

Charles Baran

Copyright ©2024 Line By Lion Publications
www.pixelandpen.studio
ISBN 9781948807456
Cover Design by Thomas Lamkin Jr.
Editing by Dani J. Caile and Michelle Levy

Author's Note

Rhoda Rage and the Goldfish Letter is a work of fiction. While the stores, restaurants, bars and locations depicted in the novel do exist, and the author highly recommends paying them a visit next time you're in town, the characters that inhabit them and the situations presented exist only in the mind of the author. Actual people have inspired many of the author's characters, but to spend time guessing would be foolish. Because he'll never tell.

For Kirk, everything, always, all the time.

And of course…Wallie.

Chapter One

Tuesday - 8am - Wilton Manors, Florida

SHIT. Rhoda could not believe it. It was only eight o'clock in the morning. Who the hell is up that early in this town? It's Wilton Manors for God's sake, not Century Village Senior Community. Wilton Manors! Gay party capital of the USA. Rhoda's eyes scanned both sides of Wilton Drive. Not a single goddamn parking spot in sight. She turned her head forward and panicked. The Honda Civic in front of her was practically coming through the windshield. She hit the brakes hard. The iced coffee she had just gotten from Stork's flew out of her hand and hit the edge of the dashboard. It landed bullseye between her legs, soaking her jeans and the light gray upholstery of her brand-new Subaru.

The cars in front of her had come to a complete standstill. Up ahead, at the intersection of Wilton Drive and NE 22nd Street, Rhoda could see the flashing lights of Officer Phillip McConnell's patrol car. A small but curious crowd of gay men and two middle-aged lesbians wearing matching peach polo shirts stood on the corner intently watching whatever had just happened. Phillip McConnell, a blonde and blue-eyed thirty-five-year-old happily married father of twin boys and plain old "Phil" to everyone in the Manor, walked along the row of cars directing everyone to turn around. As he approached the Subaru, Rhoda open her car window and leaned out.

"Hey, Phil. What's going on?"

"Oh, hey Rhoda. A nasty hit and run. Salvatore D'Angelo was knocked down crossing the street. He was walking Gooch."

"He okay?"

"He will be. His knees and elbows are a mess, but he's on his feet. Doesn't want to get in the ambulance. He can be stubborn that one."

"Did he see who did it?"

"He said it was a red van but didn't get a plate number. You better turn around and take 5th if you're in a hurry."

"Na, I'm meeting Jimmy at his place. I'll find a spot. How are the boys?"

"Just turned seven. A handful."

"I bet."

ଓ

Rhoda made a U-turn and pulled into the parking lot at Georgie's Alibi. The Alibi's mid-morning barflies hadn't started arriving yet, and the chances of someone backing into her shiny scratch-free car were nil. Even so, Rhoda decided it was better to find a spot at the far end of the lot in front of Chic Optique, the trendy eyeglass emporium where she had recently spent her entire paycheck from her last show at the Alibi on a pair of pricey Tom Ford sunglasses.

She stepped out of the car and looked down. There was no disguising the twelve-inch coffee stain. Versace. Two hundred bucks. Damn. And she had just cut the tags off too. Oh well, no time to do anything about it. She started crossing the street on her way to Jimmy's apartment when a familiar voice stopped her dead in her tracks.

"Hey Rhoda!"

Rhoda groaned. This was not a good morning to run into anyone, and especially not Ashanti. She needed to stay focused; get to Jimmy's, pick up the wig, and scram back home in time for her nine-thirty call with Apple tech support. Rhoda turned around and waved, hoping that would satisfy Ashanti and she wouldn't run after her. She was wrong.

"Rhoda wait! Hold up!" Ashanti, a five-foot-four robust full-figured gal and not the lightest on her feet, bounced across the parking lot like a poorly thrown bowling ball heading down the alley to the pins.

Rhoda tapped her foot impatiently, waiting for Ashanti to reach her, mumbling words of encouragement under her breath. "Come on, girl. A few more feet. You can do it."

With the wind knocked out of her, Ashanti arrived at her destination. She grabbed Rhoda's arm to steady herself and doubled over to catch her breath, sucking in gobs of air.

"What's up Ashanti?"

Unable to speak, she held up an index finger. Now eye level with Rhoda's crotch, she gasped when she saw the stain. "Jesus Christ, Rho! What the hell happened to your jeans?"

"I heard Animal Crackers are made from real animals, and I peed my pants."

Ashanti jumped back as if Rhoda were contagious. "They are?"

"No Ashanti. They're made from flour, eggs, and sugar. I just spilled my coffee. That's all."

Ashanti looked relieved. "Oh, good. For a minute there I thought I'd have to move to… uh, Germany."

"Move? Germany? What does that—" Rhoda had no time for Ashanti's non-sensical logic. "Look hon, I'm late. I'm meeting Jimmy to pick up—"

"Jimmy? He just left."

"What?" Just like that, Rhoda's morning went from bad to worse.

"Yeah, I saw his car heading down the drive. Right before old man Sal got hit. Who could miss that jalopy of Jimmy's? A real clunker." Ashanti was right. Jimmy's 1987 Nissan Sentra was a jalopy. It had 300,000 miles on it, a missing rear bumper, one taped-on side mirror, and the tires were bald.

His car might be a wreck like many things in his personal life, but when it came to wigs, Jimmy was perfection, a magician. He did the wigs, and sometimes the makeup, for all the top drag performers in the Manor, Rhoda Rage included. The girls on the drive called him "The Queen of the Tease." All of Rhoda's iconic drag looks were on point thanks to Jimmy; Trailer Park Tammy, Anna Phyllaxsiss, Bette Yurass, and her most famous, Angie O'Gram. Jimmy had just finished Rhoda's wig for her new extravaganza at the Alibi, and she was dying to see what he had created. The show was going to be her biggest and her best one yet, the highlight of her twenty-year career working the drive. Set to premiere in two weeks, on November 20th, her sixtieth birthday, the poster displayed in the window of every shop and bar along the drive announced *Rhoda Rage's HOLE Story.*

AND SHE NEEDED THAT WIG!!

Rhoda discreetly checked the time on her iPhone as Ashanti dove headfirst into a long-winded story about God-knows-what, interrupted only momentarily by the blare of the Holy Cross ambulance racing down the block with Salvatore D'Angelo in it. Thanks to Officer Phil's efficiency, the traffic had dispersed, and the small group of curious gays had moved on. As the siren faded in the distance, Wilton Drive returned to the lazy and quiet block it normally was at 8am on a Tuesday morning.

"Let me start over."

"Huh?"

"I said, let me start over. That stupid ambulance interrupted my story."

Rhoda forced a smile to mask her annoyance. She was annoyed that she had spilled iced coffee all over her brand-new jeans, annoyed that Ashanti had cornered her, and most of all, annoyed that Jimmy had forgotten their appointment and wasted her entire morning. As Ashanti began her story again, Rhoda's gaze wandered over Ashanti's right shoulder. Across Wilton Drive, the two middle-aged lesbians in matching peach polo shirts who had witnessed the hit and run were walking Gooch, Sal's fluffy, white Pomeranian—presumably dog sitting while Sal got checked out at Holy Cross. Seeing Gooch happily trot along Wilton Drive made Rhoda think about Wallie, her two-year-old toy fox terrier that she had left behind when she ran out of her condo to make her appointment with Jimmy. She wished she had brought him along. Wallie, the joy of her life, could always cheer her up.

As Ashanti's voice droned on, something else across the street caught Rhoda's eye. A strange man was standing in front of To The Moon, Wilton Manors' popular gift shop. Rhoda squinted her eyes behind her Tom Fords and studied the figure. Something about the odd way he stood there made Rhoda keep her eyes locked on him. He was facing the store window but not looking at any of the merchandise. He kept glancing left and right, right and left, over and over again as if concerned that he was being watched, which, of course, he was, by Rhoda Rage from across the street. Rail thin and slightly disheveled, he might be homeless or at the very least someone down on his luck. He wore a bulky, tan trench coat with large patch pockets, which was extremely unusual attire for 85-degree Florida weather. Unaware that Rhoda's eyes were on him, he fished a key out of his coat pocket, unlocked the front door of the shop, took one more look around, and quietly slipped inside. Who was it? It wasn't Sarge, the owner. And Sarge didn't have any sales help. Even if he did, Sarge never opened the store before ten. That was two hours away.

"Do you think I shouldn't have given it to her?"

"Huh?" Rhoda hadn't heard a single word of Ashanti's story.

"I said, Wen hit me up for a hundred bucks. And I gave it to her. Do you think I shouldn't have given it to her?"

Rhoda was tired of hearing about Ashanti's ex-girlfriend Wendy borrowing money from her. Every week it was the same sad story, only the amounts were different. Twenty bucks. Fifty bucks. A hundred bucks. She truly did feel sorry for Ashanti but didn't want to get sucked into the drama.

"Look hon, I've got to get going. I need to track Jimmy down and get home. My MacBook calendar doesn't sync with my iPhone and I'm a mess with computer stuff."

"Oh."

Rhoda could tell Ashanti was hurt. "Come to the Alibi on Saturday and we'll hang out after the show, okay?"

Ashanti brightened at Rhoda's invitation. She liked being friends with a star, even if it was only a Wilton Manors drag queen.

After giving Ashanti a quick peck on the cheek, Rhoda hurried across the street hoping to get a closer look at the stranger who'd gone into Sarge's store. After all, he had a key, and it wasn't Sarge or anyone she knew. And Rhoda knew everyone in Wilton Manors.

Rhoda removed her sunglasses and pressed her nose up to the store window. It was hopeless trying to see past all the kitschy merchandise Sarge had crammed together on the other side of the glass; the RBG coffee mugs, the *Golden Girls* jigsaw puzzles, the Kitty Kat Clocks, the Mae West Christmas tree ornaments, and the huge, inflated pool float in the shape of a martini glass. Whoever this guy was, he didn't turn on any lights. Rhoda pulled the door handle. Locked. Could he have left? Impossible. Rhoda was certain she hadn't taken her eyes off the shop even for a second while Ashanti babbled on about Wendy. Convinced the man was still inside, Rhoda tapped on the door. If he answered, she'd make up some story about needing to speak to Sarge, or she'd inquire about a gift she was thinking of buying for a fictitious niece or a nephew. In any case, she'd get an up-close look at the guy, and maybe even find out his name. But Rhoda's tap went unanswered. Never one to give up, Rhoda made a mental note to swing by later and speak with Sarge.

In the meantime, she needed to get on with her day. She looked across the street. Seeing that Ashanti had gone back inside Java Boys, she hurried to her car. Her cell phone told her it was exactly eight-thirty. She'd be home in plenty of time for her call with Apple. She even had time to stop by Stork's for a new iced coffee.

Rhoda pulled out of the Alibi's parking lot and hung a sharp right to Dixie. With the push of the gas pedal, she went from zero to forty, racing away from Wilton Manors and not realizing it was now her turn to be watched. The sallow man in the tan trench coat with the large patch pockets stood in front of To The Moon watching the shiny Subaru vanish in the eastern sunlight.

Chapter Two

Palm Aire - Twenty-Five Minutes Later

RHODA'S mood lightened as she turned off Powerline Road and on to the landscaped drive that led to her Palm Aire townhouse. She loved Palm Aire. The buildings with their '70s retro-vibe, the spectacular views of the golf courses, the heated swimming pools, and most of all the quick ride to Wilton Manors. Palm Aire was paradise, her Tara, her Valhalla. Rhoda smiled as she drove past the tennis courts, recalling the day Frank, her realtor, had shown her the place.

"Honey, have I got a condo for you! A real bargain!"

As filtered sunlight made playful patterns on her windshield, she started singing "Home" from *The Wiz*. Dante, the cute gardener with the toothy grin, gave her a friendly wave. Rhoda stopped the car and rolled down the window. "Hello Dante. Those impatiens sure are pretty."

"Thanks Ms. Rage. I just hope the iguanas don't eat them."

"Let's hope."

"Hey, watch out for speeding cars."

"What?"

"Drivers around here are getting crazy. When I pulled up, I almost got hit by some idiot racing out of your parking lot."

"Thanks for the heads up, Dante. And thanks for the keeping the place so beautiful." Rhoda continued her drive through the lot, enjoying Dante's colorful display of newly planted annuals, singing as she passed the geraniums lining the walkways. "When I think of home, I think of a place where there's—GODDAMN IT!"

There it was. Unapologetically spread out before her eyes, a five-foot iguana was sleeping in the middle of Rhoda's designated parking spot. Rhoda honked her horn twice then once more to signal she meant business. The lethargic creature slowly raised its head and looked at the car, irritated that its pleasant mid-morning siesta had been rudely interrupted by the honking. Languidly it inched its way to one side of the spot. Rhoda seethed. Was the iguana purposely trying to drive her crazy by taking its time? Rhoda pressed down hard on the steering wheel, letting out one more earsplitting honk. The iguana didn't care. In fact, it stopped moving altogether and turned its head and stared at Rhoda for a full sixty seconds.

"MOVE. YOU. MOTHERFUCKER!"

Rhoda hated losing her temper. Swearing like a trashy drag queen at the Pickle and Spice in North Miami Beach was not her style, but a girl could only take so much stress. Rhoda stared back, determined to win the competition. Curiously, the iguana's bumpy green flesh reminded her of the disheveled man outside To The Moon. His skin wasn't green but it sure was a sickly pale yellow and it hung off his face like a wet paper towel. Why did he have a key? Only Sarge had a key. Well, Sarge and Ben Glasser, the landlord. And unless Ben had shaved his beard and lost fifty pounds, that man was definitely not Ben. Who was he? Rhoda knew everyone in the Manor, and everyone knew her. Officer Phil called Rhoda the "unofficial mayor of Wilton Manors," a nickname she liked. Whereas Topher Stevens, Rhoda's best friend and next-door neighbor, referred to her as the "bochinchera" of Wilton Drive, a term she hated. Rhoda was not a gossip, far from it. She was just curious, that's all. And what's wrong with that?

The iguana finally relocated to a new parking space and returned to its nap. Rhoda shifted her attention to finding her house keys in the bottom of her bootleg Gucci handbag. As her hand dug among the loose change, three shades of lipstick, an eyebrow pencil, Publix receipts, and a birthday card for Jimmy that she forgot to mail, she taxed her memory to recall details about the mysterious man outside To The Moon. One, he was skinny. Very skinny. She could tell, even covered by a baggy trench coat, he was all bones. His face was thin, with sunken cheeks, and he had long, spidery arms and fingers. Two, his hollow face was pale. Too pale, she thought, for a Floridian. Three, he was overdressed for a humid Florida morning. The baggy patch-pocketed trench coat reminded her of Fagan from *Oliver!* What else? What else? She paused in her search and stared blankly at the iguana sleeping peacefully in the sun. The man's hair. Was it brown? Maybe. She couldn't remember. She did notice that it badly needly a trim. Yes, he was Fagan indeed! Rhoda shivered at the thought. With keys in hand, Rhoda headed to her front door, satisfied that she could remember as many details as she did. As she walked, she rattled the remnants of ice in the Stork's cup, her signal to little Wallie that she was home. Immediately the pooch's welcoming bark came from behind the front door. His mommy was back! Wallie the wonder dog! Rhoda's day would finally begin to turn around.

As she stepped up to the walkway, her sandal caught on the edge of a loose paver. "Ohhhhhh!" Down she went, dropping the plastic cup but somehow managing to save her Tom Ford sunglasses with a deft mid-air catch worthy of a juggler at Cirque de Soleil. "Son of a bitch!"

Wallie sensed something was terribly wrong and started barking frantically.

"I'm coming sweetie! I'm all right!" Rhoda had barely opened the front door when Wallie squeezed out, jumped into her arms, and showered her face with a million wet kisses. "Oh, my baby! I missed you!" Rhoda dropped her keys and cell phone on the entry table then hugged Wallie to her chest as he licked her neck. She left the front door wide open behind her and headed down the hallway to the bedroom without noticing the white envelope that had been slipped under her door.

Five minutes later, wearing a clean pair of sweatpants and her favorite T-shirt, Rhoda emerged from the bedroom feeling like a million bucks. Heading to the kitchen, she recounted the mornings' events to Wallie who trotted along behind her wagging his tiny tail and expecting a treat. "First of all, Wallie, Jimmy was nowhere to be found! Can you believe it? Not typical of Jimmy, right? He's always right on time for everything!"

Wallie let out a "woof" in agreement.

"Well, maybe he was visiting his mother. I know how much he worries about her."

Rhoda filled Wallie's bowl with water and gave him a bacon stick. She sat, head in hands, and watched him chew in ecstasy. Wallie's water bowl, a piece of once fine Lenox china, was the only thing she owned that had belonged to her mother. It had a tiny chip on the edge and the overly decorative design of interlaced gardenias was practically invisible from years of washing. Rhoda kept it as the sole reminder of her childhood. She had grown up an only child in Huntley, Illinois, a small town just west of Chicago. It was the 1960s. Her mother, Evelyn Bartlett, was an unhappy woman who took out all her frustrations on Rhoda, who was then known as Robby.

To avoid his mother's temper and the demeaning insults she tossed out like confetti whenever Robby walked in a room, he would spend his afternoons in front of the family's 13-inch Zenith color television set, escaping into the world of MGM musicals. Robby would imagine he was Cyd Charisse in *Silk Stockings* or Jane Powell in *Seven Brides for Seven Brothers*. Sitting cross-legged on the living room floor, he'd stare up at the TV screen and mouth the words to the songs. Little did he know he was practicing his future profession as one of the best drag performers in South Florida.

Once in a while, his father, a gentle man, brought home a soundtrack album from the local record store.

"*Gigi*! I love it! Thank you, daddy!"

"Dance with me, Robby!"

They swung around singing "The Night They Invented Champagne" while his mother watched disapprovingly from the kitchen doorway.

Rhoda refilled Wallie's water bowl and moved past the memory of life in Huntley, Illinois. "Time for another treat!"

Wallie's ears perked up. Treat was his favorite word. He rose on his hind legs and tap-danced around the kitchen floor.

Two years ago, when Topher convinced Rhoda to get a dog, she didn't realize how much her life would change. "Girl, your energy is all over the place. You need a furry friend to ground you, make you stay home more often. Take care of something other than yourself."

"You think so, Toe?"

"I know so, girl."

As Wallie devoured the salmon flavored biscuit, Rhoda remembered she needed to call Jimmy and find out what the hell happened to him. If he wasn't visiting his mother, well, watch out. Rhoda didn't like being ignored or forgotten. She went back to the bedroom to get her cell phone but realized she had left it on the entry table when she walked in. Heading down the hallway she noticed the front door was wide open. She started to close it but stopped when she saw the envelope wedged under the door. She picked it up and, using her house key, ripped it open. She pulled out a folded sheet of lined paper. The paper's top half appeared to have been hastily ripped from a pad. On it, written in pencil by what seemed to be a shaky hand, were the following three words:

THE GOLDFISH KNOW

Rhoda turned the paper over. Nothing was on the back. The goldfish know *what*? She looked at the envelope. Blank.

As she stared at the note her cell phone started to ring. Rhoda looked at the time. Nine-thirty. Apple's tech support was right on time. Calling Jimmy would have to wait. And so would the mysterious letter.

Chapter Three

Over Easy Does It

"BIG Molly's dead!"

"Slow down Ashanti. Slow Down."

Ashanti's call came the second Rhoda hung up with Apple. For forty excruciatingly painful minutes, forty-one to be precise, Rhoda had tried to sync her laptop with her iPhone. It did not go well. Not only was she unable to follow the simple commands that sexy-voiced Ramon from Apple had given her, she had pressed the delete key and deleted all her contacts with last names beginning with R, S and T.

"DON'T PRESS THAT KEY!" Ramon's warning had come a second too late. Frustrated, he suggested she take her laptop to the Apple store and hung up. Her temples throbbed.

"I said, Big Molly's dead!"

"How? When?"

"No, Wen wasn't there. Just me."

"No, I mean when did it happen?"

"Oh. This morning. Right after I saw you. Terry found Big Molly dead when she brought Molly her prescription from CVS. Or maybe it was Walgreens. She said Big Molly was slumped over her dining table face down in her bacon and eggs. It was a fucking mess. Eggs everywhere. Like they exploded…"

"Okay, okay, I get it." Rhoda's voice caught in her throat. Big Molly was one of Rhoda's closest friends. A confidante. She'd listen when Rhoda needed to unload after a fight with one of the drag queens at the Alibi or try out new jokes for an upcoming show. Molly never offered any advice, only an attentive ear and a piece of cinnamon coffee cake. But it meant the world.

"Rho, you still there?"

Rhoda blinked away the puddles in her eyes and scooped Wallie under her arm.

"Yeah. Yeah. I'm here. I…" Rhoda didn't know what to say. She swallowed and kissed the back of Wallie's head and rocked him from side to side.

"Everyone's all upset about Big Molly. There must be fifteen people already outside her house."

Rhoda stopped rocking. "Her house."

"Yeah, her house. Why?"

Rhoda's voice was back. Big Molly's house was directly behind Sarge's store. In fact, Molly's dining room window looked directly out at the back door of To The Moon. This meant Molly, and her bacon and eggs, were only a few short yards away from the strange man inside To The Moon. If he had left by the back door when Rhoda knocked, Molly could have seen him. The timing seemed right. Was it a coincidence? Rhoda didn't believe in coincidences, and her suspicions about the man grew.

"Is Officer Phil there?"

"Yeah. He just pulled up. That other guy is there too."

"What other guy?"

"The medical guy. The guy that comes and looks at dead bodies like on *Law and Order*."

"You mean the medical examiner?"

"Yeah. Him. He's a hottie. If you like guys, I mean."

Rhoda had met Nathanial Goodwin, the new Broward County Deputy Medical Examiner, once before, at a fundraiser for the mayor's reelection campaign a few months back. She wasn't too impressed. He seemed a bit cocky, and he dismissed Rhoda's interest in crime scene investigations with a condescending smirk, as if she were a silly old lady sitting at home watching reruns of *Murder She Wrote* and eating cheesecake.

"Who do you think is hotter?"

"Huh?" Rhoda wasn't listening. She was wondering if someone had contacted Leila Engermann, Molly's adopted transgendered daughter who was a social worker in Chicago.

"I said, who do you think is hotter? Officer Phil or that new medical guy?"

"I don't know Ashanti. Nor do I care."

"Oh."

Rhoda tried not to let her annoyance come through, but it did, hurting Ashanti once again.

"Did Terry say anything else? Did she see anyone?"

"Naw. She was pretty much in shock. Oh yeah, wait, she did say the front door was open when she came back with the prescription."

"Well, that's not unusual. Molly never locked her door. Only when she went to bed."

"No, she said wide open. And she remembers closing it when she left Molly's with the twenty bucks for the prescription."

Now that was odd. Why would the door be wide open? Unless someone had just left. Or was still inside?

"Stay there and keep an eye on the place. I'm on my way. And if you see some old guy in a trench coat with shaggy hair hanging around, call me."

"Will do, Rho!"

Rhoda hung up, grabbed her keys, and started for the door. She thought about changing her T-shirt and sweatpants but didn't want to waste time.

"Come on Wallie. Let's go for a ride."

Wallie, overjoyed that Rhoda was including him on her adventure, ran ahead to the Subaru and woke up the sleeping iguana who Rhoda assumed would return to her sunnier parking space after they left. She looked at the iguana and wagged a reproachful finger. "We'll be back!" Rhoda sped down Palm Aire Drive toward Powerline like Batman on a mission with little Wallie, her Robin, sitting on the passenger seat next to her. "Hold on Wallie! Here we go!" Rhoda made all the lights down Powerline, hung a left on Oakland Park Boulevard, then a sharp right on Andrews, taking the turn a little too fast. Wallie went flying and landed between the door and the seat with only his little nose poking up for air.

"Oh baby! I'm sorry! But Momma's in a big, big hurry!"

Chapter Four

Molly's House

MOLLY McNamara, better known as Big Molly, lived alone in a small beige brick and cement house that had two slightly crooked green metal awnings hung over the front windows. The window on the left was her bedroom window and the one on the right was the dining room. The front door was in the middle. She sat at the dining table every day, in a well-worn vinyl armchair, and ate her meals, read *People* magazine, enjoyed her game shows, and watched people walk up and down the block. From this window, she had an unobstructed view of the back doors of several popular shops and restaurants on Wilton Drive: the Myth Gastrobar, which up until a few weeks ago had been the popular Courtyard Cafe and from which Molly had all her meals delivered for the past ten years, including the bacon and eggs that she landed face down in; RockHard LoveStuff, the local sex paraphernalia shop; and To The Moon. The house stood out among the neighboring homes for its complete lack of charm and upkeep. For starters, it badly needed a paint job.

Molly's parents bought the house in 1957. Her dad had owned the local hardware store that sat on the corner of Dixie Highway and NE 26th Street, now home to the CVS where Molly got all her prescriptions filled. Molly grew up behind those brick and cement walls rarely venturing beyond Wilton Manors boundaries in her less-than-eventful seventy-five years. Everyone in town knew and loved Molly, waving to her daily as they walked their dogs or came home from work. She was famous for being the most caring and kind person in Wilton Manors, and in her younger years, the life of every party, shaking her tambourine in the center of the dance floor on Sunday nights at the Alibi. The crowd of concerned neighbors that now were gathered outside her house attested to the fact that she would be greatly missed.

Officer Phil and Nathaniel Goodwin were standing on the shrubless patch of dirt in front of Molly's house when Rhoda pulled up. An ambulance was parked in the driveway, which let Rhoda know Molly's body was still inside.

"Rhoda! Twice in one day! I had a feeling you'd show up."

"Hi Phil. So, what happened?"

Nathaniel Goodwin folded his arms across his chest and chuckled. He didn't like discussing details of his work with a busybody. How dare she walk up and ask what happened, as if Goodwin and Phil were working for her? "Appears to be a heart attack. Right Nate?"

Goodwin smirked and offered the smallest of nods.

"Is that so, Mr. Goodwin?" Rhoda addressed him formally, not out of respect, but to keep him off balance. Make him squirm. She didn't care for the way he stood there with arms folded, nose in the air; it reeked of Ivy League superiority. He seemed to be closing the case pretty quickly—too quickly for Rhoda's taste. "Mind if I take a look?"

Goodwin's eyes darted to Phil. Phil didn't notice the glance, but Rhoda sure did.

"Go ahead if you want to. Nothing smells funny about this one. Well, maybe the bacon and eggs." Phil laughed at his own joke and poked Goodwin with his elbow. "Funny, right. Bacon and eggs. Get it?"

Goodwin rolled his eyes and turned his attention back to Rhoda. She gently placed Wallie on the arid, dusty ground and pulled out a pair of surgical gloves and blue booties from her bag. As she bent down to put the booties on, Rhoda caught the delicious scent of Angel's Trumpet, the nine-foot shrub that grew untended on the side of Molly's house. The fragrance was intoxicating.

"I should cut that thing down before it takes over the house," Molly lamented when Rhoda asked one day if she could take home some branches.

"What's it called?"

"Angel's Trumpet. My father planted it when I was a girl. Every fall when it bloomed my mother would open the windows and let it fill the house. It sure does smell pretty."

Rhoda pulled on the gloves. "Angel's Trumpet."

"What?" Phil couldn't make out what Rhoda had said.

"Oh, nothing." As she headed into the house, she took one final deep inhale, held it, and smiled. Phil and Goodwin trailed behind her.

Just inside the door, Rhoda stopped and turned. "I heard the front door was wide open when Molly was found by Terry. Is that true?"

Phil nodded.

Rhoda turned to Goodwin to check his reaction but all she found was annoyance. "You dust the doorknob for prints, Phil?"

"Didn't think it was necessary, Rho. Nate said it's just a heart attack, so I figured why bother."

Goodwin gave Rhoda a long hard look. "That's right. Petechial hemorrhaging around the eyes, her lips are blue. Heart attack. I'm ninety-nine-point-nine percent sure of it."

Rhoda's smile was loaded with sarcasm. "Yes of course Mr. Goodwin, I guess it does seem that way, *but what about that point-one percent*?" She glanced at the doorknob, then back at Phil, who suddenly looked like a guilty schoolboy who hadn't done his homework.

"Well, maybe I should dust for prints. Can't hurt."

Rhoda, winning round one, moved slowly into the living room, her eyes carefully scanning everything around her. Wallie stayed close to her side with his nose to the threadbare orange carpet. She reached the archway leading to the dining room and stopped. Across the room was Big Molly, just as Terry had found her, slumped over the dining table, one arm dangling towards the floor, the other extended outwards across the table. Her right cheek, covered in egg yolk, rested on her breakfast plate, eyes wide open, a shocked expression on her face. On the table was a white CVS bag containing the prescription. Rhoda walked into the room studying Molly's face and the position of her body. She turned and looked at the room from Molly's point of view. Over the years, she had spent many afternoons at that dining table next to Molly's mother's treasured china cabinet, enjoying takeout burgers from the old Courtyard Cafe or a cup of Molly's strong coffee. If anything was out of place, Rhoda would spot it.

Molly's dead eyes followed Rhoda around the room. Corpses didn't make her uncomfortable. Once, when she was eight, she waited in a classroom with her dead third grade teacher, Mr. Belder, while the other students ran for help. Her steely demeanor was on display now, and Goodwin took notice. Even Wallie didn't seem to mind. He sniffed the floor around Molly's chair, sniffed Molly's slippers, sniffed the chair legs, sniffed the wastebasket. Sniffing, sniffing, sniffing. He even walked up to Goodwin and sniffed his shoes.

"Sorry about that Mr. Goodwin. Sometimes I think Wallie's got a little bloodhound in him."

Goodwin smiled uncomfortably and took a step back. He wasn't fond of little dogs.

Rhoda headed down the hallway to the kitchen but stopped abruptly at the sound of Wallie's barking coming from the dining room. Rhoda spun on her heels. "What Wallie? What is it?"

At the far end of the room Wallie was growling at an extension cord that was unplugged from the socket. The cord led to a floor lamp that stood next to the dining table. Rhoda knew the cord very well, having tripped over it many times on her visits. Rhoda kept telling Molly how dangerous it was and that she should move it, but Molly wouldn't hear of it. Too much trouble, she'd said. Molly never moved it, and the lamp was never, ever, unplugged.

Goodwin's eyes were cemented to Rhoda as she studied the cord. She turned around and looked at the front door, slowly moving her gaze from the door to the living room into the dining room, stopping at the cord. She realized that someone coming through the house in a hurry, possibly even running, could have snagged their foot on the cord and pulled it out of the socket. The open door suggested running. Rhoda walked over to the floor lamp and looked down at the carpet. A circular impression in the carpet indicated where the lamp usually stood. It had been moved a few inches to the right.

Rhoda took a few steps around the lamp, and scanned the brass pole. She was directly behind the lamp, staring at a big dent in the lampshade, when Officer Phil walked back in the room. "This lamp fell." Rhoda's declaration made Phil stop dead and look around the room. He couldn't tell where the voice came from. "Over here Phil. I said, this lamp fell. And somebody stood it back up."

Goodwin moved closer to the lamp noticing the dent in the shade. He extended his hand.

"Don't touch it!" She instantly regretted snapping at Goodwin. She didn't like him and knew he felt the same about her, but she needed him and had to keep things civil. An adversarial relationship at this point would make it harder to find out what really happened to Big Molly. "Sorry. Too much coffee this morning." Rhoda bent down and looked up inside the shade. Inside was a handprint. It was smudged and dirty, but a handprint all the same. Rhoda held up her right hand and hovered it over the imprint. It didn't fit. Then she held up her left hand. It fit. But something was off. It appeared that the person only had three fingers on his, or her, left hand.

Rhoda was about to mention this but held back. She didn't want Goodwin seeing everything she saw. Not at this point. She didn't think he had anything to do with Big Molly's death, she just wanted to gather the facts quickly and keep moving. "Did anyone check the back of the house?"

Phil shook his head.

"Well then, what say we take a look?"

Rhoda, Phil, and Wallie headed down the hallway. Goodwin followed a good ten feet behind, taking a final look at the lamp before he left the room. They stood in the doorway to the kitchen staring at the back door. It was wide open. Rhoda wasn't surprised but acted the part.

"Well, watta ya know!"

Goodwin peered over Phil's shoulder. "Gentlemen, whoever paid Big Molly a visit didn't stay very long. Oh, by the way Phil, did you dust the front doorknob for prints?"

Phil looked worried. "Yeah. I did."

"And?"

"There weren't any. None at all."

Rhoda looked at Phil, then at Goodwin. "No fingerprints on a doorknob? That seems odd. Come on Wallie. Let's go. It's time for your walk. Oh, and Phil, while you're here, better dust this back knob for prints too. Even though I'm pretty sure you won't find any."

Wallie let out a "woof" and off they went.

Chapter Five

Outside Looking In

"WHAT'D ya find Rhoda? What'd ya find?" Ashanti ran up to Rhoda the second Rhoda's foot stepped over the doorway. For thirty minutes she had paced in front of Big Molly's house, straining to catch a glimpse of the blurry figures of Rhoda, Phil, and Goodwin as they'd moved from room to room behind Molly's dusty, curtainless windows. Ashanti felt it was her duty to update each onlooker as to what was happening inside, whether they wanted to hear it or not. Each time she told her tale, it grew more and more fictitious, embellishing it to the point of implausibility. "That's Big Molly's house. She's dead."

"How did she die?"

"Don't know exactly. But it looks like -

Heart attack

Murder

Suicide

An overdose

Left the gas on

Hit her head on the table

Gunshot wound to the heart."

Rhoda grabbed the sleeve of Ashanti's T-shirt and steered her away from the house. "Ashanti, I need you to do me a favor."

"Anything Rho."

"Call Terry and ask her if… when she went in Big Molly's house, if she tripped on a cord or knocked anything over. Okay? Will you do that for me?"

"Was something knocked over?"

"I didn't say that. I said, just call her and ask if she tripped or knocked anything over. Oh, by the way, it was a CVS bag, not Walgreens, and Terry left the bag on the table."

"I'm on it, Rho!" Ashanti pulled out her cell phone. "Siri, call Terry."

Rhoda ripped the cell phone out of Ashanti's hand. "Not here! Somewhere quiet."

"Sure Rhoda. I get it. Don't want to lay all our cards on the table…" Ashanti leaned in and lowered her voice conspiratorially, like a spy in a cold war movie, "…or give our hand away or smile when the chips are—"

Rhoda cut her off. "Ashanti, listen to me. I'm heading around the corner to see Sarge. Give me a call and let me know what Terry said." Rhoda handed Ashanti back her cell phone, scooped Wallie up, and hurried down the block as Phil and Goodwin stood shoulder to shoulder watching Molly's body being loaded into the ambulance. Just as Rhoda turned the corner and disappeared out of sight, Goodwin's phone began to ring.

Chapter Six

Fly Me To The Moon

"HELLO? Anyone here?" Rhoda stood at the counter looking down the narrow aisle for Sarge. It was almost half-past ten and although the store was open, the lights were still not on. The minimal eastern sunlight coming through the front window had created long shadows on the floor, but it wasn't enough for Rhoda to see farther than a few feet down each row. Like the front window, the store was a hodgepodge of merchandise. Every inch of shelf space, and most of the floor space, was crammed with colorful gift items; children's toys, puzzles, racks of greeting cards, coffee mugs, rolls of wrapping paper, and shelves and shelves of stuffed animals of all types that took on a sinister presence as they stared down at Rhoda in the dim light. The only noise was the constant *tick tok tick* from a Kitty Kat Clock on the wall behind the cash register. The cat's large, black and white eyes looked left and right as the clock ticked away the time. Rhoda suddenly felt the presence of someone behind her. She turned and jumped seeing a rubber head of

Donald Trump attached to the top of a toilet brush. Above the display was a sign that said, "Make My Toilet Clean Again." Taking a step back, she bumped into a rack containing glass jars filled with candy that Sarge sold by the pound; gummy bears, jellybeans, Sno-Caps, rainbow all-day suckers, cinnamon Red Hots, and licorice sticks. The clock struck the half hour and let out a long, plaintive *meowwwwwwww* as the kitty's eyes rolled in their sockets. Rhoda looked up. The ceiling faintly glittered in the reflected sunlight coming through the window. It was breathtakingly covered with magnificent Christmas tree ornaments in all shapes and sizes. She had seen these ornaments many times before and was always amazed at the magical effect they created. Normally they would have sparkled all the way down the aisles of the store. But now, in the absence of light, the spectacular display looked dead and lifeless.

Rhoda's gaze zigzagged across the ceiling, taking in each ornament. Many were in the shape of famous people and cartoon characters, Mickey Mouse, Donald Duck, Little Mermaid… She spotted Lady Gaga, Elton John, Andy Warhol, and one that resembled Joan Crawford but the lips were all wrong. Then something strange made her stop. Tucked in a dark corner where the ceiling met the wall were some hideous ornaments. It surprised Rhoda that Sarge would choose to display them, when all his other merchandise was so fabulous— Joan Crawford's lips notwithstanding. They were cheap looking, plastic, no sparkle at all and not the delicate, handblown glass that all the others were made of. Surely no one would buy them. There must have been at least twenty. Perturbed by their lack of charm, she started counting them but stopped when she felt a strong tap on her shoulder. Her heart stopped.

"Rhoda. What are you doing here?"

She whipped around. It was Sarge, with beads of sweat dotting his forehead. His breathing was labored, as if he had just finished hauling a grand piano up eleven flights of stairs. She looked down and gasped. In his right hand he held a bright yellow box cutter with the blade fully extended. She took a small gulp and smiled. "Hello, Sarge."

He didn't reply. He just stared vacantly into Rhoda's eyes. Something was wrong. His usual smile wasn't there. His mouth was tight-lipped with a slight quiver at the corners. Rhoda looked for signs of her old friend, but the face staring back was alien to her. She wanted to speak but had no idea what to say. She had known Sarge for over thirty years and they had shared laughs, heartbreaks, and hurricanes together. His real name was Brent Wilson, but everyone called him Sarge because he looked like one, stocky and bald with a big, gray, bushy mustache. He'd be perfectly cast in the 1960s war film, *The Dirty Dozen*. He even owned a sergeant's uniform and wore it on Saturday nights at The Eagle, a leather bar a few doors down from To The Moon. Other nights, however, he stayed home in Dania Beach with his cat Mr. Wiggles watching old episodes of *Designing Women* on his Danish modern sofa.

Sarge stepped closer to Rhoda, the eyes of the Kitty Kat Clock moving left to right on the wall behind her, as if warning her to run. The open box cutter in Sarge's right hand lifted towards Rhoda's arm, coming within inches from her left shoulder. Rhoda locked eyes with Sarge waiting for him to strike. Her peripheral vision could see the shiny blade travel past her shoulder. She held her breath. Then she heard a "clink" and exhaled, realizing Sarge had laid the box cutter on the glass countertop. "What brings you by today, my dear?"

"Uh—just wanted to stop in and say hello." Rhoda held Wallie tightly to her chest and nervously stroked his head, fighting the urge to bolt out the front door. "I was around the corner at Big Molly's. You heard about that?"

"Oh." Sarge's smile faded. "So sad. So sad. Well, it's always great to see you, Rhoda." Sarge walked behind the counter and started tidying up, moving things around unnecessarily, all the while avoiding Rhoda's eyes. "Stop by again soon. Holiday time is around the corner and I'm getting in a bunch of new items. A full set of John Waters dinnerware. Service for eight. Divine!"

Rhoda kept her eye on the box cutter laying within Sarge's reach on the counter. The impulse to leave had subsided and she remembered what she came for. "I see you're already unpacking new stuff."

"What? Oh yes, a few boxes came in. Nothing terribly exciting. Just an order of Tootsie Rolls. They're still popular, you know.

Rhoda didn't want to talk about Tootsie Rolls. She wanted to talk about Molly. "Yes, it is so sad what happened this morning."

Sarge picked up the box cutter, blade still extended, and sprayed the counter with Windex.

"Yes indeed, poor Sal. I hope he'll be okay. Is someone watching Gooch while he's at Holy Cross?"

"I'm sure someone is. But I meant Molly."

"Oh yes, Molly. Terrible. Terrible. A heart attack. What a shame."

Rhoda studied a Ruby Slipper keychain that hung on a hook next to the cash register. "Yes, a heart attack. It certainly appears that way."

Rhoda wondered how Sarge had gotten this information. Even on the gossipy streets of Wilton Manors, it seemed a bit fast for details about Molly's death to be circulating. She had just left Goodwin talking to Phil in front of Molly's house. She nonchalantly looked around to make sure someone wasn't lurking in one of the shadowy aisles. There was a clear path to the front door in case she needed it. She was about to ask Sarge why he hadn't turned on any lights, but when she looked back around, Sarge was gone. Rhoda tried calling his name, but her voice stuck in her throat. She leaned over the counter and looked down as Sarge popped up, causing her to let out a frightened, "Ohhhhh!"

"Sorry. Dropped the Windex."

Rhoda swallowed and stroked Wallie who had begun whimpering, sensing the danger. "Mind if I ask who told you it was a heart attack?"

Sarge stopped mid-spray and looked up at nothing. "Let me see… let me see… who was it? You know, I can't remember."

Can't remember my ass, Rhoda thought. It only happened two hours ago. Sarge's obvious obfuscating was the catalyst Rhoda needed to find her fearlessness. "Sarge, was anyone here this morning before you opened up? In the store, I mean."

Sarge, caught off guard by the question, knocked over a jar of pencil erasers shaped like rainbows. "Whaaa…t?"

"I saw someone go into the store this morning. It was around eight-thirty. Skinny guy wearing a trench coat. He had a key and let himself in."

Sarge took a deep inhale before he replied. "In here? No, I think you're wrong. Are you sure it wasn't Rock Hard next door? That place always has new people coming and going."

"No. No. Pretty certain it was your place."

Rhoda could see Sarge struggling to find an explanation.

"Oh, I know! It must have been someone from Ben's office. I have a leak in the back that I wanted him to fix. I'll call him later and ask. Thank you for letting me know."

Ben Glasser, Sarge's unpleasant landlord, didn't have an "office." He was a one-man operation and too cheap to hire an assistant. There wasn't any leak. What was Sarge hiding? Rhoda knew questioning him further wouldn't amount to much. She decided it was better to let Sarge think he had succeeded in deceiving her. "Of course, Sarge. I'm sure that was it. Someone from Ben's office. Sorry to have mentioned it. You have a good day now. Oh, and don't forget those Tootsie Rolls."

"Tootsie Rolls?"

Rhoda nodded at the box cutter.

"Ah yes, the Tootsie Rolls!"

Rhoda waved and headed out the door. Sarge waved back and when she had gone, he took a paper towel and ran it across his damp forehead.

As soon as Rhoda stepped outside, her phone rang. She looked at the caller ID and sighed. "Robin?"

There was no reply. Only silence on the other end. Then came a faint faraway voice, unfamiliar, harsh and scratchy. Rhoda struggled to hear it.

"Hello? Robin is that you? Who is this? Hello? Speak up!"

Still harsh and scratchy but now a louder harsh and scratchy, Rhoda recognized the caller.

"Rhoda? Darling? Yes, it's me. Robin! Your drag-sister. Listen sweetie, I simply cannot, I mean absolutely cannot, host Drag Bingo tonight at Spencer's. I have completely lost my voice and it's taken everything out of me to even make this call. My throat is on fire, darling! On FIRE! The entire Wilton Manors Fire Department and their long-long-looooonnnng hoses couldn't put out the red-hot blaze that's burning inside my throat. It's taken everything out of me to even make this call. Have I said that already? I have, haven't I. BUT. IT'S. TRUE! Can you cover for me tonight darling? Please. Pretty please with rhinestones on top? I'll owe you oodles and oodles of chocolates and flowers and whatever the hell you want."

For someone whose throat was on fire, she sure could gab. But that was typical of Robin Kradles. Everything she did was a big performance. Robin Kradles was a drag queen and Rhoda's number one competition in the clubs along Wilton Drive. Sometimes they were friends, sometimes they were not. It depended on who was drawing the bigger crowd.

"I don't know, Robin. I've got so much going on. Can't you call Sunny Conditions? I feel bad no one ever hires her, and she could use a break."

"No one hires her for a reason, darling. Have you stood near her? Deodorant is not found in her medicine cabinet. No, no, no. She'll have them all running down the block for five-dollar tacos at Tulio's. Please darling, help me out. I need you!"

Rhoda, against her better judgement, agreed. She knew if she didn't, Robin would keep calling and would wear her down until she said yes.

"Sure, sure, hon. I'll cover. I just feel bad for Sunny."

"Oh, grow up. It's a drag eat drag world. Sunny should move to Daytona Beach with the rednecks. I heard they have a bar up there that's gay every other Wednesday. That's perfect for her. It takes her two weeks to put her lashes on. You're divine! Oh, and darling, it's a nautical theme, so dress like a mermaid or a goldfish or something wet…"

GOLDFISH! Rhoda had forgotten all about the mysterious note that was waiting for her back at home. What the hell was that about? Could it be connected to Molly's death? And the skinny trench-coated man?

Robin's rasp brought her back. "Rhoooooo-da! Are you still there darling? Or did you hang up on me? Too excited to talk?? Rhoooooo-da…"

I'm here. What time should I be there?"

"Sex."

"What?"

"Six, darling. Six!"

"Why so early? It doesn't start until seven."

"To set up the cards and shit."

Rhoda checked her watch and groaned. It was almost eleven. There was lots to get done before "sex." She had to get home, feed Wallie, come up with a "nautical" outfit, pick her music, think of jokes, do her makeup, pick out a wig… A WIG! Where the hell was Jimmy?

"I gotta go."

"Of course, darling. Thanks again. I just know you'll—"

Rhoda hung up on Robin mid-sentence. She scooped Wallie into her arms and bolted around the corner to her car.

Chapter Seven

Back Inside To The Moon

"YOU handled her pretty well."

Sarge, still holding the damp paper towel, opened his eyes. He saw the unpleasant face of Stretch Breezy who was still wearing the large tan trench coat with the patch pockets that Rhoda had seen him in that morning. He and Sarge had been in the back of the store unpacking boxes when Rhoda had paid her little visit. But it sure wasn't Tootsie Rolls they were sorting. Hidden behind a display of Play-Doh in the farthest aisle, Breezy had overheard every word of the conversation.

"She's a smart one, I'll give her that, but I don't think you gave away any candy from the candy store. Ha-ha." Stretch opened the gummy bear jar and helped himself, popping two in his mouth and the rest in the pocket of his coat. He chewed noisily with his mouth open, the blue and green gummy bears sticking to his bottom teeth. Sarge took the opportunity to offer his advice.

"You know, everyone listens to Rhoda. And if she suspects something is going on, it won't be long before we have Officer Phil and possibly even the Feds coming around here asking questions. I can't afford to lose my business. Or worse, go to jail."

"If that's the case, Sarge, we'll just have to handle her like we handled her friend."

"Molly?"

"No. Her other friend. The wig guy."

"Jimmy? What have you done to him?"

Breezy picked up the box cutter and wagged it close to Sarge's face, nicking his nose with the tip.

"Ouch. That hurts." Sarge backed up to the wall, out of Breezy's reach. Directly over his head the Kitty Kat Clock struck eleven. *Meeeeooooooowwwwww.*

Breezy let out a long, evil cackle. "Wouldn't you like to know what I did to him. Now, get back there and keep counting before we get another interruption. Oh, and put the closed sign on the door."

"What? I can't do that. People will wonder why the store is closed. What will I tell them?"

"Tell them you were so upset about that fat bitch dropping dead you had to go home. If she was that well-liked, people will certainly understand." Breezy treated Sarge like a baby and he spoke to him in a condescending way. It made Sarge angry. He wasn't a fool. He hated Breezy and wished he could jump over the counter and stab him. But Breezy held the box cutter. He was always in control. But that didn't stop Sarge from lashing out at the despicable creature that was ruining his life.

"You shut up! Molly was loved. More than you'll ever be, you disgusting little pig turd. If I had a gun, I'd, I'd, I'd…"

Breezy leaned over the counter and slapped him hard. Tears came to Sarge's eyes as he rubbed his cheek. "You would what? Huh? What would you do? I'll tell you what you would do. You'll put the fucking closed sign on the door and get back there and keep working on those boxes."

Chapter Eight

Molly's House Redux

"HI, this is Jimmy, and if it's six inches or longer you know what to do. If it's not, just hang up and don't bother calling back. Ha-Ha-Ha. Bye."

"Jimmy, it's Rhoda. Where are—"

"I'm sorry, the mailbox is full and is not accepting messages at this time. Goodbye."

Rhoda threw her phone across the front seat of the car, barely missing Wallie's balled up body lying on the passenger side. He shot up and bolted to the safety of the car floor. Rhoda stared at Molly's front door. She dug her fingernails in the steering wheel and, as Wallie's whimpering pierced her eardrums like hundreds of hypodermic needles, her chest tightened and she took in quick short breaths. "Will ya calm down Wallie, we'll be home in a few minutes."

Through her windshield, she could see Jimmy's two-story apartment building on the next block. If he was home by now from wherever-the-hell-he'd-been, she could pick up the wig. She got out of the car and walked a few feet looking down the block for his beat-up jalopy. Her phone start ringing inside the car, and she sprinted back to grab it, but the passenger door was locked. Wallie, back up on the seat, barked at Rhoda through the window. He jumped toward the glass, knocking the phone to the floor. She ran to the other side, opened the door, and dove headfirst into the car. Spread across the seats, the gear shift pressing painfully against her ribcage, her hand searched the floor of the car. Too late. She found the phone and dialed the number back. "Hi Ashanti. What's up?"

"I just called you!"

"Yes. I know. I'm returning your call. What's up?"

"Good news! I spoke to Terry."

"And? And?"

"Oh, right. She said she didn't knock anything over. When she saw Molly slumped over the table with eggs all over her face she ran back out. She said she almost threw up but didn't. She said she dry heaved. You know. When you think you're gonna throw up, but nothing comes…"

"Okay, okay, I get it. What else?"

"Oh, then she called 911."

"Thanks Ashanti. That helps."

"It does? Wow. That makes me feel good, Rho, real good, that I can help you solve this…"

"Ashanti, I have to go. Thanks again."

"Oh, Rho! One more thing! I almost forgot. I told Terry that you saw the CVS bag on the table, but she said she didn't leave it on the table. She said she dropped it on the floor. She never went anywhere near the table. The eggs almost made her throw up, but she didn't."

Rhoda grabbed the dashboard and pulled herself up. "Really. Now that's interesting."

"Well, not really. Terry has a real weak stomach. We went to see *Mission Impossible* and Terry got sick watching Tom Cruise hang from that plane."

"Ashanti, great work. I gotta go. You've been a big help."

"Look at us Rho, we're a regular Smith and Wesson!"

"Smith and Wesson?"

"Yeah. The detectives."

Rhoda thought. "Oh, you mean Holmes and Watson."

"Yeah. Right. Well, adios, Rhoda!"

Rhoda dialed Officer Phil's cell phone, a number she used only in an emergency.

"Hey Rhoda. What's up?"

"Phil, I'm sorry to bother you but I want to ask you a question. Were you the first person to arrive at Molly's this morning?"

"Yes. Yes, I was. Well, I mean, I pulled up the same time as the ambulance. So, we arrived together. But… wait. That's not right. Goodwin was there. As I got out of the car, he came out of the house. I didn't think much about it, but now that you mention it… it seems odd that he got there first."

"Uh-huh. One more thing Phil. Do you remember seeing a little white bag on the dining table? The kind from a pharmacy?"

"I dunno. I think I did. Maybe. But can't be sure. There was a lot of stuff on the table. Does it matter?"

"No, not really. Thanks Phil."

Rhoda started to hang up, but Phil stopped her. "You don't think Goodwin is connected to any of this, do you? Are you thinking he knocked over that lamp?"

Rhoda knew it wasn't Goodwin, the handprint didn't match. All his fingers were intact. "No, he didn't knock it over." She started to say more but held back. "Phil, do me a favor and don't mention any of this to anyone. Okay? I want to figure a few things out first."

"Okay, Rho. I guess it's not looking like a simple heart attack, is it?"

"I wish it was as simple as that. Thanks for taking my call, Phil."

Rhoda's frustration lifted when she realized she was making progress. Not much, but it was progress. Two of her suspicions had just been confirmed. One, Terry didn't trip on the cord and knock over the lamp and, two, it was Goodwin, not Phil or Terry, that put the CVS bag on the dining table. It had to be. Was any of this useful in finding out what really happened to Molly? Rhoda felt it was but didn't quite know how. Yet. The bigger question bothering Rhoda was how did Goodwin know to arrive first? Did someone tip him off? Was it the person who knocked over the lamp? Rhoda absentmindedly tapped her dashboard, wondering what answers she could find behind those dirty windows. She checked the time on her iPhone. Eleven fifteen. "Come on, Wallie. Let's have another look."

Rhoda turned on the ignition and quietly drove her Subaru down the block towards Jimmy's building, out of sight from Molly's house. She found an empty guest spot, parked, and with Wallie in her arms she headed back, glancing left and right as she walked. The block was empty. She quickly headed up Molly's cracked walkway to the front door and turned the knob. It wasn't locked. She pushed the door slightly, and before slipping inside, she turned and looked at the back of To The Moon. Sarge still had not turned on any lights. Rhoda, not seeing the pair of eyes watching her from behind the black void of the store's tiny rear window, went inside Molly's house and quietly closed the door.

Chapter Nine

Broward County Medical Examiner's Office

GOODWIN held his phone to his ear and listened. His expressionless face stared at a wall chart that listed the signs and symptoms of biliary disease.

"You set for tonight?"

"Yeah. Sure."

"Don't sound so excited."

Goodwin didn't care how he sounded and offered the caller no contrition. He wanted to keep the relationship strictly business. Breezy wasn't a friend. "What time?"

"Sunset's at five-thirty so be there at six."

"Same place?"

"Same place."

Goodwin hung up without saying goodbye. He stared down at the surgical tools laid out on the utility table in front of him. His stomach soured and a foul taste filled his mouth. How the hell had he let himself get mixed up with someone like Breezy?

On the stainless-steel table, half covered by a crisp white sheet, lay Big Molly, all 274 stiff pounds of her. He wished he was dead. Or was somewhere else. This way he wouldn't have to…

"Excuse me Doctor, I'm stepping out for lunch. Can I pick something up for you?"

A weak smile was all he could offer, hoping Kate wouldn't notice his distress. Goodwin liked Kate. He depended on her. She was an excellent worker, meticulous, never a mistake or a typo. Thirty-two, pretty, with a devoted husband and two small children. Goodwin envied her stable life. "No. Thank you Kate. I'm not very hungry and I want to get this autopsy done. I'll have the notes to you later."

Kate glanced over at the dead body. The overhead fluorescent lights made Molly's skin appear translucent, slightly blue. She shook her head. "Poor lady. Heart attack?"

"Yes. Fairly certain."

"Well, text me if you change your mind."

"Why would I change my mind?"

Kate stared at him. Goodwin had never snapped at her before. Clearly, he had not realized what she had meant.

"About lunch. If you change your mind, I mean."

"Oh. Yes. Of course." Goodwin noticed the look in Kate's eyes as she left the lab. He had never spoken to her that way and wondered if this would mar their relationship. It didn't matter if it did. Kate would hate him when she found out. He stared down at the incision on Big Molly's chest. He was responsible for this. Not entirely, but he did play a part.

As Goodwin worked on Molly's body, he recalled the unpleasant events of the morning. It all began with Breezy's phone call telling him to "get his ass over to Big Molly's house before that pretty boy cop got there." He instructed—no, he demanded—that Goodwin "straighten up the place and get rid of any evidence." Breezy told Goodwin he had "knocked over a floor lamp" but that he had stood it back up. He didn't mention it was unplugged. Goodwin didn't notice nor did he think to check that Breezy had put it back in the same spot. That snoopy drag queen sure had a good eye. The only thing Goodwin had time to do before Phil and the EMTs arrived was to wipe Breezy's prints off the doorknobs with a Kleenex that he still had in his pants pocket. He dug his hand down deep, quickly pulling it out and tossing in the trash can by the door. Then he remembered something else. He had also put the CVS bag on the table. Was that wrong? He looked up and thought about it. It wasn't a big deal. Was it? He couldn't resist picking it up off the floor when he walked in. Anyway, Breezy did say to "straighten the place up." Now he regretted doing it. There was something else. The lampshade. He was sure Rhoda had noticed something about the lampshade, but she didn't say what. Goodwin fought the urge to scream. He kicked the stainless-steel cart holding the surgical instruments, which sent it rolling to the other side of the room. His hand trembled holding the twelve-inch trocar that he was trained to use honorably in a respected profession. He had worked so hard, long hours, a prestigious degree from Johns Hopkins, internships. Four years as a forensic pathologist in Cuyahoga County Coroner's Office in Cleveland, Ohio. A brilliant future ahead of him. For what?

Goodwin adjusted his face shield and leaned over Molly's body. He focused his attention only on the job in front of him, shutting out the sound of Breezy's voice, the look on Rhoda's face as she announced, "this lamp fell," the jab of Officer Phil's elbow, "bacon and eggs, get it?" For the next hour, alone in the quiet of the lab, Goodwin would be the best prosector on the planet. When he finished, he switched off the overhead light, placed the scissors, forceps, and retractor in the instrument tray and raised the white sheet, covered Molly, and wheeled the examination table to the refrigerated wall. His preliminary determination of Molly's cause of death was correct. Myocardial infarction. An ordinary heart attack.

"I'm back."

Goodwin turned around. Kate was standing in the doorway holding a white bag high in the air. Her familiar smile had returned to her face.

"I picked up a chicken salad on rye just in case."

Goodwin returned the smile and felt the world brighten just a little. Maybe this wouldn't be so bad for him. "Thanks Kate. I am a bit hungry after all." He removed the blue latex surgical gloves and tossed them in the hazardous waste receptacle. Kate held the door for him as he passed through to the hall, dropping his lab coat in the laundry bin as he walked. Kate took a quick glance around, noting the work to be done after lunch—sterilizing equipment, sanitizing the counters, replenishing the supplies. She looked down at the little stainless-steel trash can next to the desk where Goodwin kept his notes. There was only one thing in it, a single rumpled Kleenex lying at the bottom, which she'd get later. Kate switched off the lights, shut the door, and followed Goodwin as he headed to the staff lounge.

Chapter Ten

Blow Softly and See

RHODA stood in the living room grateful to be alone. She was certain there were things she missed earlier when Goodwin's eyes were laser focused on her back. The house was hot and stale. Rhoda couldn't breathe and she felt sweat accumulating at the base of her neck. Wallie stood panting by her side, desperate for cool water. Rhoda switched on the overhead fan, which created a minimal warm breeze that provided only the smallest amount of relief. The single air conditioner in the house was a tiny window unit in the bedroom that Molly rarely turned on. It felt strange being there. Unfamiliar. Big Molly's absence made the house seem tomblike. A kaleidoscope of broken shadows and fractured light spread across Molly's dusty furniture and discolored walls. Rhoda wondered if she should give up, forget about it. Molly died of a heart attack. Leave it at that. She had no idea what she was looking for. Why bother? She had so much to do to get ready for tonight. Suddenly Drag

Bingo seemed a lot more important than a good friend's death. But something was compelling her to stay. So, she did.

Rhoda, fastidious, neat, and organized, never particularly enjoyed being in Molly's house with its forty-year-old orange shag carpet that hadn't been vacuumed since who-knows-when. As much as Rhoda loved her friend, she was not a fan of her flea-market decor or her lack of housekeeping skills. It was a sense of duty to a good-hearted person that made her ignore the musty odors and put on her latex gloves and blue booties and get to work. Even Wallie overlooked the dust bunnies and helped, sniffing under chairs, behind doors, and along the greasy baseboards in Big Molly's kitchen.

Rhoda walked over to the dining table and studied the items laid across its surface. Along with the CVS bag set closely to the edge, there was a stack of junk mail, an electric bill showing an amount due of $62.59, a pair of binoculars that she had never seen before, four mismatched placemats, and seven well-read *People* magazines. On the placemat in front of Big Molly's chair, the chair Molly sat in from the time she woke up to the time she went to bed, was Big Molly's last meal, a half-full cup of coffee and a Styrofoam container with the remnants of Molly's breakfast; two eggs sunny side up, turkey sausage links—never patties!—and rye toast, dark to the point of being burnt and buttered on both sides. It was the exact same breakfast Molly had delivered every morning promptly at 7:30am by either Fred or Jose, her favorite waiters from the Courtyard Cafe who had been kept on when it recently reopened as Myth Gastrobar, the back of which could be easily seen from the front window.

Rhoda stared at Molly's empty chair remembering the many times she had visited, sharing dirty jokes or talking about Molly's health. Molly's door was always open, literally, to her friends and neighbors. Several times Rhoda chastised Molly for not locking it. Molly's response was to brush it off as nonsense.

"Why should I lock it? I got nothing to steal. And keeping it unlocked saves me from getting up and down all the time to open it. It takes me a full minute to get out of this chair!"

Rhoda circled the table and sat down in the swivel armchair and rubbed the old, worn, drab brown vinyl with her fingertips. The discolored stuffing that had found its way through the cracks on the armrests brushed uncomfortably against her forearms. She swiveled to the right and tippy toed back to the left, scanning the expanse of the room. Aside from the floor lamp that had been knocked over and repositioned, everything else appeared status quo. Rhoda looked at the front window and saw the back entrance of the Myth Gastrobar. Slightly to the right, she could see the back doors of To The Moon and RockHard LoveStuff.

"Huh." Rhoda started to reach for the pair of binoculars, when a cold wet nose poked her leg. She looked down. "You need a walk Wallie?"

Wallie stared back up with a #2 pencil in his mouth.

"What have we here?" Rhoda patted Wallie on the head and took the offering. She looked at the faded lettering, the chewed eraser. Pressing her finger against the needle-sharp tip suddenly reminded her of the mysterious letter waiting for her back home. Wasn't that letter written in pencil? Suddenly possessed, she began flinging the magazines and junk mail until she found what she was looking for. "Ah-hah!"

Hidden under Molly's placemat was a simple yellow legal pad with the top page torn off. As if holding a scared scroll from ancient Egypt, Rhoda ran her hand delicately across the paper. Trancelike, she moved to the front window and examined the pad closely, running a finger along the uneven tear at the top. Moving her fingertips further down the page, her touch detected a faint imprint. She squinted and held it to the light, but could not make out any of the words.

Defeated, she stared mindlessly through the window at the back of To The Moon. A half-second later Rhoda was racing down the hall to the kitchen with Wallie barking at her heels. She flung open Molly's kitchen cabinets and began searching wildly. She pushed aside the long-neglected remnants of Molly's pantry; old bottles of pancake syrup, boxes of Rice-A-Roni, swollen cans of kidney beans, a box of hardened raisins. Hiding behind a dusty, unopened, five-pound bag of flour, she found her prize, a box of Hershey's cocoa powder. Not touched in years, the cocoa was still powdery.

"This will do." She found a tablespoon and dug it deep into the powder. Then, standing over the sink, she shook the spoon over the pad, lightly dusting the imprint. Rhoda took a deep inhale, circled her lips and blew across the page. She smiled as she read the words.

THE GOLDFISH KNOW

The start of a neighbor's lawn mower gave Rhoda such a scare that she knocked over the box of Hershey's on the counter. She grabbed a dish towel and started brushing the powder into the sink when she noticed the time on Molly's microwave. She panicked when she saw it was three-nineteen.

"That can't be right."

She fumbled for her cell phone. It was only one o'clock. She dropped her phone, the pencil, and legal pad into her tote. She groaned at the powder covering the sink and instinctively reached for a sponge but remembered Robin's command to be there at six. "Come on Wallie. Let's go." She flew out the door and looked up. Dark clouds had moved across the neighborhood. They added an oppressive gloom to Molly's desolate-looking front yard. "Quick Wallie. In the car."

She drove fast. Her thoughts hopped from the legal pad to Drag Bingo, from Jimmy to Goodwin arriving first, Molly's sink to nautical outfits she had no time to make. A car cut her off. In her mental rerun, when the cocoa spilled, there was a sound. Just as she blew. Cocoa everywhere. What was it? A duck. Yes. She had heard a duck. She was running out the door. Wallie was barking. It was in the living room. Somewhere. Not on the table. But she'd heard it. Quack, quack, quack. What was it?

Chapter Eleven

Let's Brake for Bingo

THE nine parking spots in front of Spencer's Corner were already taken when Rhoda arrived at six fifteen. Not only was she late, now she had to drive around looking for a goddamn parking space. As Rhoda circled the block, her anger grew. Aside from a handful of chocolate covered cashews, she hadn't eaten a thing all day. Her feet hurt and her head throbbed from running back and forth to Wilton Manors investigating Molly's death and trying to find Jimmy. She wished she had told Robin Kradles 'no', that she was far too busy to host Drag Bingo. Robin had other friends she could have called. The fabulous Miss Bouvee or talented Susie Toot were great gals and would have been happy to fill in. Why did it always have to be her? And why did she always say yes?

On top of that, Rhoda hated the idea of being seen in the ridiculous "nautical" outfit she had concocted in less than an hour. After ransacking every closet, box, and drawer in her townhouse, all she could come up with were a few yards of aqua tulle, some gold ribbon, and a bad wig. Certainly not on par with Jimmy's glamorous creations. With Wallie sitting on the bedroom floor wondering if Rhoda had forgotten his dinner, Rhoda ran around with a pair of scissors in one hand and a can of spray mount in the other. She wore an old, peach, tie-dyed leotard that she found in the bottom of a banker's box stored behind a chenille bedspread on the top shelf of her closet. She draped the aqua tulle over the leotard, looked in the mirror, and ripped it right off. After a few snips with the scissors, she tried again. She gathered the material and placed it over one shoulder letting it run down her back and front, then, using a wide sequined purple belt she cinched the netting at the waist, pulled and tugged around the belt, and fashioned the tulle into a big, flouncy skirt that ended just above her knees. Standing in front of the full-length mirror, she took the scissors and trimmed it up just a teeny tiny bit higher. Bingo! Her legs looked great. Then, cutting the gold ribbon into six-inch pieces, she strategically attached six hot pink plastic starfish to the tulle. The starfish lived in a glass bowl on a shelf in Rhoda's guest bathroom. They were a "gift" from the former owner of Rhoda's condo, and she hated them. Rhoda had forgotten to take them to the Out of the Closet Thrift Shop when she donated her unwanted clothes and bric-a-brac, but was now glad she had them to accessorize her ridiculous outfit. At five fifteen Rhoda still wasn't satisfied with her outfit so she added a few more touches. A jaunty rubber duck in a navy-blue sailor's cap sat on her shoulder in the middle of an outrageously large orange bow. Wallie whined when he saw the rubber duck, his favorite squeak toy, perched out of his reach. Rhoda had been reluctant to use it, but the outfit needed something to finish it off, and it was either that or the artificial orchid plant from her dining room table. The rubber duck had a sentimental value; Topher had given it to her one drunken New Year's Eve after she drove him home from a dance party at Club Boi in Miami. The squeak toy was his way of apologizing for throwing up on the hood of Rhoda's old car, a 2001 BMW that died one night on Andrews Avenue coming home from the Alibi.

Around her neck was a cheap souvenir shop necklace made out of large snail shells that Rhoda quickly embellished in the final minutes before she ran out of the house using purple glitter and the can of spray mount, the smell of which overpowered the interior of Rhoda's Subaru and caused her to drive the entire way from Palm Aire to Spencer's Corner with all the windows rolled down. The coup de grace was a cheap looking black wig cut in the style of Coco Chanel or, more accurately, Anna May Wong. The wig, purchased at the ABC Beauty Supply store on Oakland Park Boulevard, was a leftover from last year's Halloween party at the Alibi when she and Robin Kradles and Miss Sweet Ann Brosia did a number as "The Golden Ghouls." Needless to say, they brought down the house.

Rhoda found a spot in front of Le Patio Restaurant, two blocks away from Spencer's. As she parallel parked her car, her mood lightened, and she began singing the theme song from *The Golden Girls* with the lyrics she had written for the Halloween show last year.

> *"Thank you for being a fiend*
> *Flew on our broomsticks and back again*
> *Your skin is green, you're a witch and an evil queen"*

As Rhoda walked swiftly towards Wilton Drive a hibiscus branch snagged on the aqua tulle skirt. (Goddamnit!) Rhoda looked down and stared at the big hole on the side of the skirt. This was positively the last time she would ever put an outfit together in less than an hour or do a favor for Robin Kradles. Rhoda kept her head down. She dreaded running into anyone on the street. There was tacky and then there was *tacky.* "Please, please, *please,* don't let anybody see me," she mumbled to herself as she hurried along Wilton Drive to Spencer's.

"Rhoda! Is that you?"

Oh god. Her nightmare had come true. She looked up and saw Officer Phil coming out of Dolce Salato carrying a pizza box and a bag of garlic knots. Rhoda forgot her embarrassment when she saw how good Phil looked out of uniform. He was wearing a tight blue T-shirt that said, "Captain Andy's Everglades Adventures" and even tighter khaki shorts that showed off his well-developed thighs.

"Hi Phil. Yes, it's me and if you tell anyone you saw me in this outfit, I'll have to kill you."

"Ha-ha. Don't worry Rhoda, your secret's safe with me. I am glad I ran into you though. I've been thinking about something that happened earlier today. When we were at Big Molly's."

"Oh really? Do tell." Rhoda drew closer, interested in hearing what Phil had to say but also enjoying the smell of the garlic knots.

"Sorry about the smell. Tuesday night is pizza night. The kids love it."

Rhoda's stomach growled. Hunger and exhaustion overwhelmed her. She leaned against a *South Florida Gay News* kiosk to keep from passing out. Damn that Robin Kradles. She better be sick. Really, *really* sick.

"You okay?"

"Yeah. Yeah. I'm fine. So, what's up, Phil?"

"This morning, after you left, when I dusted the back doorknob for prints Goodwin hovered behind my back watching me like a hawk. It was just creepy. That's all."

Rhoda nodded her head in agreement. "Thanks for letting me know Phil. How long has Goodwin been in town?"

"Eleven months. He started at the beginning of the year."

"Uh-huh." Rhoda looked down the block and saw a handful of people heading into Spencer's. "I gotta go, Phil. I'm late. I'm hosting Drag Bingo at Spencer's."

"Drag Bingo. Ha-ha. That's funny."

"Well, it's not too funny when you're the host and you haven't eaten all day."

"Wanna slice?"

Rhoda thought of taking Phil up on the offer but there was no time. Plus, she could only imagine the disappointed look on his kids' faces when they saw a slice missing from their Tuesday night treat. "I'll take a rain check! Thanks Phil!"

And just then, as if on cue, an eardrum shattering thunderclap exploded above them and fierce Florida rain pounded down. In a matter of seconds everything, including Rhoda's tulle skirt and Phil's pizza box, was drenched.

Chapter Twelve

Pressing Play

AS the lightning flashed and the thunder rumbled over Wilton Manors, the front door of Spencer's Corner flew open with a smack. Every head turned and looked. Rhoda Rage stood in the doorway, a big purple and aqua sponge, a puddle of water accumulating at her feet. Benny, the hot Latino bartender, shrieked with delight. "Rhoda! Chica! You look amazing! Let me get a towel. And my fishing pole!"

Rhoda, managing a weak smile, dripped her way across the floor towards the bar, her right arm extended to the rag that Benny waved in the air like a surrendering sailor. She dried her wig by using gentle little pats over the synthetic black tresses. She didn't dare take it off. Underneath, her own hair looked scary, pinned up and hastily shoved under a wig cap. "Thank you, Benny," she mumbled from under the towel. "It's not one of my best creations but it will have to do."

"Oh, it is your best, mami, it is. I love the duck." Benny let out a little "quack, quack" to be funny and Rhoda froze. She slowly raised her head and peered out from under the white cloth.

"What did you say?"

"I said it is one of your best. I love the duck."

"No, no. The other thing."

"Other thing? Oh. You mean the quack, quack. Like a duck. Quack, quack. Ha-ha."

That sound. It brought her right back to Molly's living room. She had heard it when she was leaving. She was certain. Quack, quack. Where had it come from?

Benny leaned over the bar and gave Rhoda a peck on her wet cheek. He reeked of Danger Pour Homme, the sexy cologne that he liberally applied just before his shift. The intoxicating scent made Rhoda forget all about Molly's house and the quacking sound. As he fluffed the orange bow on Rhoda's shoulder, Rhoda stared dreamily at his curly black hair and well-developed biceps.

"There you go. Nice and fluffy. Ready to be a star."

Rhoda handed him the wet cloth and turned towards the stage. Alfredo, the serious and efficient manager of Spencer's Corner, and Benny's on-again off-again boyfriend was on top of a six-foot ladder adjusting the banner that announced in big yellow letters DRAG BINGO EVERY TUESDAY NIGHT AT 7! Underneath, in smaller letters, the banner also announced HOSTED BY ROBIN KRADLES. Rhoda rolled her eyes. Robin was such a publicity whore. She had insisted on her name being on the banner when she agreed to host the weekly gig. Alfredo wasn't too pleased and didn't want to accommodate her request. When the day came that Robin Kradles didn't host Drag Bingo anymore—and that day would certainly come; drag queens were always coming and going like mice in a church basement—he'd have to cough up another $250 for a new sign.

"Hello, Alfredo. I'm here."

A clap of thunder punctuated her greeting.

"Hola, Rhoda."

Alfredo, absorbed in his effort to get the sign perfectly straight, didn't turn around to notice Rhoda's outfit or that he would need to mop up the trail of water she was leaving behind. Rhoda, however, did a double take when she saw that Alfredo had bleached his black hair totally blonde and had it cut in a trendy new style.

"Wow, Alfredo. Your hair looks amazing. I never thought you were the type to make such a drastic change!"

"Thanks Rhoda. Sometimes the quiet types can surprise you. People are not always who they seem to be. Right?"

"You're right about that, Alfredo." Alfredo's remark reminded Rhoda of what Phil had said just minutes ago outside Dolce Salato about Goodwin hovering over him as he dusted the back doorknob at Molly's house for prints. Why would a Deputy Chief Medical Examiner do that? Yes, people are not always who they seem to be.

"The Bingo cards are in a box in the back. You need help?"

"I think I can manage, Alfredo. Thanks."

"Does this sign look straight to you?"

"It's the straightest thing in the place," Rhoda responded and headed to the back room.

While Alfredo put the ladder away, Rhoda set up the table on the tiny square stage, arranging the wire basket containing the Bingo balls, the microphone and an old laptop that Alfredo always kept under lock and key when there wasn't a show. Rhoda found her memory stick in the bottom of her handbag and plugged it into the laptop. Her precious memory stick contained all the music tracks for the songs she performed, and, unlike her handbag, it was very organized. There were folders for each type of music: show tunes, standards, disco, pop, and country. Rhoda had a great voice with a decent range and sang all her songs live to tracks. She hadn't lip synced in over twenty years. Each song on her memory stick was arranged and recorded by her fabulous musical director, Billy Treaco, and they cost Rhoda a fortune. Billy lived with his Greek husband Yannis in a little house in Margate filled with tons of Madonna memorabilia that Yannis would sell online on eBay. The three of them had become great friends over the years. Billy's skill at arranging music was just as brilliant as Jimmy's talent for styling wigs. There was a folder labeled "Icons" that contained tracks for songs made famous by her favorite divas: Judy Garland, Barbra Streisand, Bette Midler, Cher, and her ultimate favorite, Shirley Bassey. There was even a folder labeled "Camp" that contained an assortment of songs so outrageous they couldn't be classified into any of the other categories—songs from Yma Sumac, Marlene Dietrich, Doris Day, and the Andrews Sisters, among several others. Rhoda scanned the list of titles deciding what to play. Of course, she'd open with her "welcome" song, the song she opened all her shows with and for which she was famous. It was a rap song that she had written the lyrics to years ago when she was just starting out. Billy polished it and set it to music.

I'm Rhoda Rage, I'm number one

Sit back, relax, the show's begun

I'm a little bit Judy, Bette, and Shirley

Don't miss a sec cause you got here early

Let me hear you say

PARTY!

PARTY!

So, clap along and if your able

Put hands in the air not on the table

'Cause I'm Rhoda Rage, I'm number one

Sit back, relax, the show's begun

Let me hear you say

PARTY!

Since Drag Bingo was less about the *Bingo* and more about the *Drag* it was important to give the crowd, a fifty-fifty mix of locals and out-of-town tourists, a show they'd remember. It also drew a fair number of straight women who sometimes brought along their hunky husbands as designated drivers. Rhoda, firmly believing in the show business mantra to "play to the crowd," decided to go right into Reba McEntire's "Pink Guitar" but with her own lyrics of course.

I love to play, I love to rock,

Sometimes I like to bottom, sometimes I like to top

So, come on down, to my cookie jar

I'll dress in black like Johnny Cash

With a pink sports-bra!

Yes, Reba would be perfect for Drag Bingo.

Rhoda glanced around at the crowd and counted only six empty seats. Then she checked the time on her cell phone. It was ten minutes to seven and she still had to put all the Bingo cards and markers on the tables and run to the bathroom for a quick hair, makeup, and costume check. Still feeling slightly damp, she was worried what she'd see in the mirror when she looked.

The "early birds" had occupied all the tables directly in front of the stage. Rhoda had another nickname for the folks who showed up early: "wanna-bees." They were folks that wanted to be on stage but didn't have any talent. They sat up front in the hopes that the star of the show would single them out and have them come up on stage. That's how she met Ashanti. Five years ago, when Ashanti moved to Wilton Manors, she became a "Rhoda Rage groupie." She attended every single one of Rhoda's performances, sometimes two a night, and she always sat right up front. After seeing Ashanti in the audience night after night, Rhoda decided to have her come up on stage. And once Ashanti got up there, Rhoda couldn't get her off. "What's your name hon?"

"Ashanti. Ashanti Turna. Like Tina Turner but with an A at the end instead of an E-R!" Ashanti then burst into an off-key, a cappella rendition of "What's Love Got To Do With It." The crowd laughed as she strutted around the stage. "Wanna see me vogue?"

"Uh… no sorry dear, I'd rather see you pony back to your table."

Ignoring Rhoda and egged on by the crowd, Ashanti started voguing as Rhoda gently guided her back to her seat. The five years since they met had gone by quickly and as annoying as Ashanti was, they had become good friends.

Rhoda scanned the tables checking out tonight's group of "wanna-bees." She spotted a cute twenty-year-old twink wearing a Kylie Minogue T-shirt. "Honey, can you put these cards and markers on the tables for me? I gotta freshen up."

Before the kid could say "yes" Rhoda was on her way to the bathroom. Rhoda looked over at the bar and saw Alfredo pointing to his wrist. It was seven o'clock and time to start the show. She held up a finger and mouthed "one second" and bolted into the bathroom. Her reflection in the dimly lit room wasn't as bad as she'd thought. She fluffed her wig, blotted her lipstick on a piece of toilet paper, and picked a clump of mascara from an eyelash. Thirty seconds later, she was standing on stage giving Benny a signal to turn off Lady Gaga's "Poker Face." She turned on her mic, gave it a tap, and welcomed the crowd. "Hello hello! Welcome to Drag Bingo where the only thing cheaper than the drinks are the prizes. And me! I'm your hostess, Rhoda Rage! Come on in. There's a few seats left. And remember, if the chairs fill up, there's always one spot left, right up here with me!"

Rhoda winked at a handsome construction-worker-type man wearing a faded Van Halen T-shirt who had just walked in with his giggling wife. He had the look of someone facing a firing squad. He clutched his wife's hand for safety as she pulled him to a table towards the front. Before he could sit down, Rhoda shoved the microphone in his face. "Honey, why don't you tell the crowd it's showtime?"

In a barely audible voice, the man said "showtime" as his wife smiled sweetly and rubbed his shoulder.

Rhoda egged him on. "Come on honey, I know a big strong guy like you ain't shy. Let me hear you say SHOWTIME!"

"SHOWTIME!"

The crowd applauded as a big burst of lightning lit Spencer's up in a flash of blinding radiance.

Rhoda pushed the guy down in his chair. "Now shut up and pay for your wife's drinks!"

More lightning. More applause. This was going to be a fun night. Rhoda saw Benny laughing at the bar. He gave his hand a shake, letting Rhoda know he thought the guy was "hot, hot, hot." Rhoda smiled and pressed play on the laptop.

I'm Rhoda Rage, I'm number one
Sit back, relax, the show's begun…

Chapter Thirteen

Slippin' in Slippin' Out

AS the relentless rain turned Wilton Drive into a river and the furious wind blew the fronds off the palm trees outside Spencer's Corner, a mile away in an empty parking lot behind a row of vacant storefronts on NE 12th Terrace, directly across the street from the Peter Pan Diner, Nathaniel Goodwin's black Nissan SUV and a gray Honda Accord were parked side-by-side in the dark. The door of one of the storefronts opened and Goodwin, head bowed, shoulders hunched to avoid the rain, ran to his car carrying two brown boxes, each about the size of an average shoebox. As he struggled opening his car door, the window of the Honda rolled down and a flat voice floated out.

"You got all of em?"

Goodwin winced. "Yes, that's it. All five."

"Good. Have it ready by Friday." Breezy started the Honda.

"Friday? But that's only three days…"

Breezy cut him off. "Four actually. You still have tonight."

Goodwin groaned. Breezy obviously expected him to go back to the lab and start working.

"Better get going. Friday will be here before you know it." With that, he rolled up the window and pulled out of the lot just as a freight train came barreling along the tracks on the other side of Dixie Highway.

ଔ

"B 7!"

Someone in the back shouted, "BINGO!"

"I see we have a winner! Who yelled Bingo?"

"I did!" An overly excited woman waved her bingo card high in the air. When she tried to stand up, she fell right back down. From a distance of thirty feet, Rhoda could tell the woman had already consumed several of Benny's strong cocktails and wondered if she should ask her to come up to the stage or have Alfredo take her the prize. Aw, what the hell, the night had been going smoothly so far.

"Come on up here!"

The lady raced to the stage like someone who spotted a twenty-dollar bill on the sidewalk. She held onto the shoulders of people along her way and knocked into a few tables and chairs.

"What's your name, hon?"

"Mary."

Rhoda chuckled. "Honey, everyone here is a Mary. You have to be more specific." The crowd roared. Rhoda went up to the handsome guy in the Van Halen T-shirt, now three Bud

Lights in, and placed her hand on his head. "This guy's a "virgin" Mary if you catch my drift."

The crowd roared even louder. Rhoda scanned the room enjoying the laughing faces and pounding of feet. Just when she was about to turn away, she stopped. It was him. She was sure of it. The overcoat, the hair. It was the man she had seen that morning walking into Sarge's store.

"What's my prize?"

"Huh?" Rhoda, totally distracted by seeing the man come through the door of Spencer's, had forgotten all about the bingo game.

"I said, what's my prize? What did I win?"

"Oh, yeah, sure honey. You've won..." Rhoda dug around in the bag of prizes that Robin gave out to the winners, penis shaped ball point pens, a pair of handcuffs, edible underwear. Typical junk. Rhoda wanted to send Mary back to her table with a special prize, one that she wouldn't get at any other drag show, so thinking fast, she ripped off one of her hot pink starfish and handed it to her.

"Here you go! You get the first starfish! We're giving them out one-by-one! I have five more left, so five more winners! If someone wins twice, they get the duck!"

Benny let out a "quack, quack" from behind the bar and Rhoda turned around. She searched the room. Where did the man go? Had he left already? The door to the men's room opened and bright fluorescent light spilled into the bar area, silhouetting the man in the doorway. He headed to the bar, pulled up a stool, and sat down. Rhoda sighed with relief.

"Okay, everybody! Next game! Here we go! N 24!" Rhoda kept one eye on the Bingo balls and the other on the man. She watched as Benny walked over to his new customer.

"What'll it be?"

"Rum and coke."

"You want lime in that?"

"No." The man was not talkative nor polite, but Benny didn't care. He was more interested in listening to Rhoda's banter than making small talk with a stranger.

"Before I call the next number, how many Bingo virgins do I have here tonight? Come on, let me see those hands!"

Two cute twenty-something-year-old guys who were sitting on the side of the stage sheepishly raised their hands. One was blonde and the other had jet-black hair and wore glasses that made him look like Clark Kent's younger brother. Rhoda spotted the matching wedding bands and decided to have a little fun. "Where are you boys from?"

"Richmond Virginia," the one with the glasses answered.

Rhoda shouted, "Virginia boys in the house!" and the crowd applauded.

"On vacation?" Rhoda asked.

"It's our honeymoon!" the blonde said.

"Oh! We have a couple of newlyweds, folks! Let's get them up here."

The audience shouted with encouragement as Rhoda pulled the giggling boys up on stage. "Folks, I don't know if you know this, but I've heard that same-sex weddings in Virginia are not legal until they've been performed by a drag-queen-of-the-peace right here in Wilton Manors, gay town USA! So wadda you say we get these boys hitched all over again right here and now?"

"Yes! Yes!" The crowd was loving every minute of it.

"We need a bridesmaid! You, honey. In the Van Halen T-shirt."

The husband, embarrassed at being a bridesmaid, didn't want to participate, but his wife gave him no choice, shoving him off his chair and commanding him to "GO!"

"Now, we need a best man. Let's see…" Rhoda, knowing exactly what she was doing, pretended to scan the crowd. Of course, she planned on picking the mystery man at the bar. Once he was up on stage, she would subtly pump him for information; find out his name and where he was from. "You! At the end of the bar. Get up here!"

The man just stared, one hand on his rum and coke the other on his knee. Benny tried helping Rhoda out.

"Go ahead up man. It's all for fun. Rhoda won't bite."

"I'll pass. How much do I owe ya?"

Benny looked at Rhoda and shrugged his shoulders, letting her know she should move on.

"How much?" the man asked again.

"Six dollars."

The man dug a wallet out from one of the pockets of his trench coat, struggled to open it and pulled out a ten. "Keep the change."

Rhoda watched the man walk out of the bar. Her plan had backfired. Fuck. She should have waited. Let the guy settle in, have a few drinks. She could have talked to him after the show. Fuck. Fuck. Fuck. The crowd was getting impatient. They started chanting "Best Man, Best Man!" Rhoda spotted Marvin, a harmless older gentleman that she knew from the Alibi, sitting alone with his Bingo cards at a table. "Marvin honey, would you like to be our best man?"

Rhoda's frustration disappeared when Marvin stood up, bowed, and said, "It would be an honor madam."

"Okay, here we go! Everybody ready? As drag-queen-of-the-peace, I, Rhoda Rage, using the fabulous powers vested in me, now pronounce you husband and husband."

To Rhoda's surprise, Alfredo had found a track of Mendelssohn's wedding march on Spotify and played it at full volume while the crowd banged their drinks on the table and yelled, "Kiss! Kiss!"

When the impromptu wedding ceremony was finished and everyone returned to their tables, Rhoda struggled to keep things moving. Seeing the man from To The Moon had broken her concentration and she couldn't get the rhythm of the show back. All she wanted to do was run over to Benny and find out what information, if any, he had on the guy. Without jokes or ad libs, Rhoda raced through the last four rounds of Bingo. She called out the numbers so fast, the crowd couldn't keep up. People kept shouting, "Slow down, slow down," as they searched for numbers on their Bingo cards, their markers poised in the air. She tossed the remaining starfish to the winners in the audience, not asking anyone to come up on the stage. As for the rubber duck, she gave that to the cute couple from Virginia. By 8:25 the night was over.

"Bye everybody! Thanks for coming. Get home safe. Roll up those windows. And watch out for alligators and snapping drag queens." Rhoda turned off her mic and headed to the bar.

Alfredo grabbed her arm and stopped her mid-route. "Wow Rhoda. That was quick. We usually go till nine. You in a hurry?"

Rhoda batted her eyes and looked innocent. "It's such an awful night. This rain! I wanted to get everyone out of here and home safe."

Alfredo's glare clearly told Rhoda he wasn't pleased. The storm was moving north and only a light drizzle misted the streets outside. He could have sold a dozen more drinks in that last half hour. Rhoda began mumbling apologies, but Alfredo cut her off. "Don't worry about it, Rhoda. Just remember for next time. Okay?" He handed her five twenties and started removing the empty glasses from the tables.

"Hey mami. You on speed?"

Rhoda ignored Benny's remark. "Who was that guy that came in?"

"What guy?"

"The guy I tried getting up on the stage. You know. When I did the best man part. He left right away."

Benny stared at Rhoda, thinking hard.

"You know, Benny. The guy in the coat."

"Oh, that guy. I dunno. I never saw him before. I don't think he was even gay."

"Did you get his name?"

"No. Didn't ask. Didn't say. He wasn't too friendly."

"Did he pay by card?"

"No. Cash. Good tipper though. Left me a four-dollar tip."

Rhoda, deep in thought, stared at the door, tapping her nails on the bar as Benny rinsed out glasses.

"Hey, why are you so interested in him? He didn't seem like your type."

"I'm not. Not in that way. Look, I can't talk about it. But if you remember anything about him, anything unusual, or something he said, let me know."

"Okay, chica. Hey, you wanna drink? On the house."

"I'll take a seltzer. Put some cranberry and pineapple juice in it. Thanks."

"Ah. A Robin Kradles special coming right up. She's probably enjoying one right now in Key West."

Rhoda's head snapped. "What?"

"I said a Robin Kradles special. That's what she always drinks. Miss Robin is probably enjoying one right now in Key West."

"Key West? She's not in Key West. She's home sick."

Benny laughed. "Is that what she told you, mami? Is that how she got you to host Drag Bingo? No, mami. Miss Robin is feeling just fine. She went to Key West. She's using her raffle prize that she won last year at…"

"Scandals," Rhoda interjected through gritted teeth.

"Right! Scandals. A free stay at The Island House. That place is fabulous. And clothing optional! But so expensive."

Rhoda remembered the night Robin won the raffle. They were just about to leave Scandals Saloon, when the evening's emcee, Tammy Whynott, called the last of the raffle prizes, one free *weekday* night at The Island House, gratuities not included. "L30269"

"Come on, Robin. Let's go." The noise and cigar smoke at Scandals had given Rhoda a headache and she was rushing Robin towards the exit when Tammy called the number again. "L30269."

"Wait Rhoda. I think that's my number." Robin dug around in her bag for the ticket.

"Why do you think it's your number?"

"Because darling, the number ends in 69, my favorite position! I'd never forget that! Here it is."

Tammy Whynott repeated the number one more time.

"Anyone have L30269?"

Robin screamed, "IT'S ME!"

Rhoda closed her eyes and massaged her temples as Robin raced to the stage to claim her prize. Now she'd never get out of there. Robin—a freshly minted grand prize winner— would be impossible for the rest of the evening. Rhoda checked the time on her iPhone and groaned so loudly when she saw it was nearly midnight that the overweight man in the assless chaps standing next to her leaned over and asked if she was alright.

"I'm fine," she snapped. She had been trying to leave for over an hour an hour, but Robin, who had come in Rhoda's car, had insisted on staying until all the raffle numbers were called. Robin begged Rhoda to drive her because she hated driving at night and hated driving even more when she had her two-inch false eyelashes on and couldn't see beyond the steering wheel. Rhoda had thought about suggesting Robin take an Uber home, but Robin—being so cheap—would have complained about it for weeks.

"Yes, Benny. I remember very well." Rhoda took a sip of her "Robin Kradles special." She was annoyed, not so much with Robin's duplicitousness, she'd deal with her later, but more annoyed at herself for letting the mysterious man in the trench coat slip away.

"Excuse me, Miss Rage?"

Rhoda turned around and saw the honeymoon couple from Virginia. "Oh, hi boys. You have a good time tonight?"

They beamed bright shiny faces and nodded their heads. "Oh yes. You were so fabulous. Can we take a picture?"

"Of course, fellas. My pleasure. One minute." Rhoda, suspecting she looked faded and tired, took out her ruby red lip liner, color "Vicious," and gave her lips a much-needed boost and freshened-up her beauty mark. The blonde of the two pulled out his iPhone and extended his arm, struggling to get the three of them in the shot.

"I'm so bad with selfies. Plus, I've got a broken thumb."

Rhoda hadn't noticed it before, but the guy's thumb was in a splint. Rhoda called Benny over to help. "Benny, can you take this for us. This boy's thumb is busted!"

Benny grabbed the phone and moved a little to the left then back a step to the right, trying to get the perfect shot. "Okay, you guys lean in tighter around Rhoda. Move your head down, now up a little, there's a glare on your glasses. Rhoda, move a little to the left, and you with the busted thumb, put your hand on Rhoda's—"

Benny lowered the phone and stared at Rhoda.

"What's wrong Benny?"

"There *was* something."

"Huh?" Rhoda didn't understand what Benny was taking about.

"Chica, you asked me if there was anything I remembered about the guy. There was. His left hand only had three fingers on it. Three fingers and a thumb."

Benny held the camera back up. "Now smile and say cheese!"

The boys from Virginia yelled "cheese!" as Rhoda, face frozen in shock, whispered "three fingers" just as the flash went off.

Chapter 14

Midnight Oil

SQUISH. Squish. Silhouetted in his blackened office window, Nathaniel Goodwin stared down at the parking lot of the Broward County Medical Examiner Building looking at the only car in the lot, his car, which he had purposely parked under a streetlight so as not to draw attention to it. As he thought about moving it to a dark corner—was he wrong about the light not drawing attention to it?—he shifted his weight from foot-to-foot making an audible squishing sound in his semi-new Nike Vaporfly two-hundred-and-sixty-dollar sneakers, which encased his feet like two wet dish towels. Squish. A sudden flash of brilliant lightning illuminated his dimly lit office spotlighting the plain brown box sitting dead center on the desk behind him. The nondescript box was minimally larger and only slightly heavier than the box that had recently contained the pair of wet Vaporflys but much more valuable. Goodwin wiggled his toes in the cold spongy socks still thinking about the car. Should he move it? The box on his desk contained a kilo of pure, uncut cocaine, street value forty thousand dollars. It would be worth almost double once Goodwin cut it (the process of diluting cocaine with additives such as procaine, creatine, and boric acid). For Goodwin's services Breezy would pay Goodwin eight thousand dollars cash. Per kilo.

Goodwin glanced at the clock on the wall. Three minutes past nine. Even though he was the only one in the building—was he?—the box sitting innocently on his desk caused his intestines to cramp. He squeezed his ass cheeks tight and shifted his weight from foot to foot. Squish. Squish. He stared at his car sitting in the halo of the inky black pavement to see if the other four boxes on the floor behind the driver's seat were visible. He should move it. A drop of warm sweat escaped from his left armpit and slowly ran down the inside of his shirt stopping unpleasantly at his waistband. He took a sip of the flat tasting water that had been on his desk since morning and rolled his car key around the bottom of his pants pocket. Three days? What was Breezy thinking? He pulled the key out and pointed it at the car, quickly hitting the lock button. He exhaled when he saw the lights flash on and off. Good to double check. He turned and looked at the box. He took another sip. Even if he recruited someone to help, it would take more than three days. He shuddered at the thought of having Kate, his innocent assistant, pulled into such an unsavory assignment. Goodwin's intestines cramped again and he let out a foul gas. It reminded him of that day in ninth grade when he was unprepared for an algebra test.

"Ugh! Nate just farted!" his nemesis Bender Murphy exclaimed. Amber and Jessica laughed and covered their faces as the teacher tried to restore calm.

"Are you okay, Nate? Do you need to use the restroom?"

Young Nathaniel, embarrassed, shook his head and slumped in his chair continuing to struggle with the math problems he didn't understand.

Goodwin left the box unattended on his desk and squish-squished his way down the hallway to the employee lounge. Before entering, he turned and looked at the telltale wet footprints trailing behind him on the pristine linoleum tiles and wondered if they'd leave a trace when dried. He opened the refrigerator and saw the half-eaten cannoli cake from last week's birthday celebration for Eston, the lab technician. The cake was left uncovered and the icing had become hard and brittle. He tossed the cake into the metal trash can making a loud "thud" when it hit the bottom. The inedible cake gave Goodwin an idea. He would dump the five boxes somewhere deep in the Everglades and keep driving, far away, somewhere, anywhere. Canada maybe. But then he remembered he hated the cold. Mexico? No. That's where the stuff came from. Breezy would hunt him down in Mexico and… Goodwin closed his eyes and leaned against the counter. He didn't want to think about what might happen to him if he didn't fulfill his part of the bargain. Bargain? What bargain? There was no bargaining about it. He had been coerced into doing it. It had gone on too long and now his options were limited. In fact, he could only think of two; disappear and start his life over with a new identity or turn Breezy and his associates in to the Feds. Either one meant the end of his medical examiner career. He had no options. Breezy had him by the balls. It was too late to get out.

Goodwin watched a helium balloon that said "Happy Birthday" float ominously around the employee lounge. The balloon had just enough helium in it to keep it hovering four feet off the floor. Goodwin felt it move toward him, stalking him, ready to pounce. He turned around, grabbed a fork from the sink and stabbed the balloon over and over again yelling "FUCK YOU FUCK YOU FUCK YOU!" He looked up. Rhoda Rage was staring at him, her mouth open, laughing. He took the fork and jabbed the face of Rhoda Rage on a flyer pinned to the bulletin board announcing her upcoming show. *"Rhoda Rage's HOLE Story at the Alibi!"* That bitch was everywhere. He ripped the flyer off the board, crumbled it up, and pressed it down into the trash can with the menacing balloon. His heart started racing. He panicked remembering the kilo of coke sitting on his desk. He ran down the hall and flung his office door open. Everything was just as he had left it. Steadying himself against the doorway, Goodwin closed his eyes and took in deep slow breaths. When he had calmed, he picked up the box and headed down the hall to the lab.

ের

Goodwin's nightmare started eight months ago on a crisp, starlit April evening over a dinner of fresh Florida Stone Crabs at Catfish Deweys with his childhood friend Tony Fasano. They had grown up next door to each other in the Baltimore suburb of Glen Burnie but hadn't been in touch since their graduation from North County High School almost twenty years ago. When Goodwin announced on Facebook that he was relocating to South Florida from Ohio, Tony, who had moved to Florida after dropping out of the local community college, sent him a message and the two were reacquainted. Goodwin was dubious about getting too close; in high school, Tony was a troublemaker and a goof off while Goodwin obeyed all the rules and tried hard to succeed. But sentimentality and a touch of homesickness coupled with Tony's persistence had won Goodwin over and the two frequently went to dinner together, most often to Catfish Deweys.

After the statuesque blonde server had cleared away the empty crab shells, Tony leaned in conspiratorially and asked Goodwin if he could do him a favor.

"Sure Tony. What's up?"

"I was wondering if, with your medical skills and all, you could cut a brick of cocaine that I got. It's raw stuff and I can't use it like that."

"You're kidding me, right?"

"No, I'm serious man. Can you help me? You've probably got everything you need at work."

"No way, Tony. I can't bring that stuff into the lab."

"Aw, come on man. It's a favor. I can't use it if it ain't cut. And you know you like a little coke now and then."

Goodwin was about to turn Tony down when the server interrupted. "Can I get you fellas another round of margaritas?"

Tony spoke for both of them. "Yeah, sugar, and bring an order of Coconut Shrimp too."

A second margarita was followed by a third. Tony, a master in the art of persuasion, kept the conversation light, not mentioning the subject again until Goodwin's eyes were sufficiently glazed over. The cover band in the bar played Tim McGraw's "Indian Outlaw" and Goodwin hummed along with a stupid grin on his face.

Tony knew the time was right to try again. "So, wadda ya say man? You gonna help me out or what?"

Goodwin, enjoying the effects of three strong Margaritas, was totally absorbed in the song and didn't hear Tony. "Dude! I love this song!! *I'm an Indian outlaw, half Cherokee and Choctaw…*"

"So?"

"So what? *My baby she's a Chippewa…*"

"The coke. Cutting the coke."

"Oh right. The coke. *All my friends call me Bear Claw…*" Goodwin kept singing, pounding the table to the rhythm and smiling stupidly at Tony.

"So? Wadda ya say?"

Tony waved his Visa card in Goodwin's face, a subliminal message that he would be picking up the tab. Goodwin, deep in the music and deeper still in the tequila laden margaritas said yes. Just like that. Yes.

"Yeah, yeah man. Okay, okay, sure. I'll do it. *Cause I'm an Indian Outlaw! Half Cherokee and Choctaw! My baby's she's a Chippewa…*"

Little did Goodwin know as he crooned along with the cover band that Tony's one "favor" was only the beginning.

A few weeks later Goodwin received a call from Tony. "Hey man! I never really thanked you for helping me out. You did really good. I had no complaints from my customers."

Customers? Goodwin wasn't aware that Tony was selling the stuff. "Uh, yeah Tony. Sure. No sweat."

"No, no man. I want to officially thank you."

"You don't have to do that Tony. Forget it."

"Dude, I got us a pair of primo tickets to the Marlins Phillies game in Miami! Memorial Day weekend!"

"Gosh Tony you didn't have to go and do…"

"Wait, wait, there's more. I booked us a suite at Casa Casuarina in South Beach! You know, Versace's place. I mean, dude, he was shot right outside."

Goodwin, who liked a grisly murder scene even more than baseball, was intrigued by the thought of sleeping in Versace's old bedroom. "Wow, Tony. That's seems like an awfully expensive way to say thanks."

"No problem, my friend. Glad to do it!" Tony Fasano was a smart operator, and he knew the twenty-five hundred for the suite and the thousand dollars for the Marlins tickets would be money well spent. Goodwin would be indebted to him for a long time. "You excited?"

"Yeah. Yeah. I am. Thanks, Tony."

After the Marlins game, over a Campari and soda at Casa Casuarina, Tony ran into two friends, Ignacio and Martin, at the hotel bar. They were brothers and told Goodwin they owned a pool maintenance company in Broward County. Goodwin, sober and in command of his senses this time, felt something strange going on between Tony and the brothers. It all seemed planned; bumping into them in the bar, the afterparty in their room, Tony's endless supply of coke, the booze, and the two women, Rini and Yvonne, who showed up at midnight and spent the night. Halfway through the evening, Goodwin determined that Ignacio and Martin were clearly not the kind of people he wanted to hang around with. They had moved to Florida in the mid-nineties from Slovakia because they enjoyed "sunshine and beautiful women." With chiseled features and muscular bodies, Ignacio and Martin looked more like male strippers than businessmen. They might have had a career in modeling if it weren't for the bad teeth, something easily noticed by Goodwin, a trained medical professional. What Goodwin didn't know that evening as he watched Tony snort line after line of coke on the marble coffee table in the twenty-five hundred dollar a night hotel suite with Rini and Yvonne sitting next to him on the midnight blue velvet sofa drinking five hundred dollar a bottle champagne, was that the drunk and obnoxious brothers, along with Tony, worked for one of the biggest coke dealers in South Florida.

A week later, after Tony's all-expenses-paid weekend in South Beach, Goodwin met the big boss, the king of the organization. Early that Thursday morning, 7am to be precise, Tony phoned Goodwin, interrupting his breakfast and the article he was reading in *Academic Forensic Pathology* entitled "Crocodile Attack Injuries - A Failed Attempt to Conceal Homicide."

"Hey dude, sorry to call so early but I need a favor."

"What's up, Tony?"

Goodwin was on his guard this time. After the drug-fueled evening in Versace's old living room, he had decided it was wise to keep a healthy distance from Tony. Sometimes it was best to leave your high school memories as just that, memories.

"Can you pick me up at the Fort Lauderdale airport? Tonight? South terminal. Baggage claim 3. The plane lands at 9:20. Park in the Hibiscus garage."

An airport pickup seemed innocent enough, so what the hell. He jotted down Tony's instructions on a paper towel. While they were specific regarding arrival time and baggage claim, Tony had purposely omitted two pieces of information, the flight number and the airline. And Goodwin, intent on finishing his article before leaving for work, didn't think to ask.

At exactly 9:19 that evening, Goodwin was standing in front of baggage claim 3 looking around for Tony. Several flights had recently landed and the baggage area was a sea of heads.

"Are you Nathaniel Goodwin?" The unfamiliar voice came from behind.

Goodwin froze. He expected to see DEA agents pointing guns when he turned around. He braced himself, swallowed and turned. A skinny, disheveled man somewhere between fifty and sixty in a trench coat and a pair of wrinkled polyester blue pants stood before him.

"Who are you?" Goodwin had no intention of confirming he was Nathaniel Goodwin until he knew who the guy was.

"I'm a friend of Tony's. You're picking me up."

Goodwin searched the crowd beyond the man's head looking for his friend then stared at the stranger for several confused seconds. "Where's Tony?"

The baggage carousel started turning. "Ah, the bags are coming through. I have to get to Deerfield Beach by ten so let's hurry."

Deerfield Beach? What the hell was going on? Before Goodwin could respond, the man disappeared into the mass of bodies surrounding the carousel. Goodwin glanced up at the arrivals and departures board and saw that the flight unloading bags onto baggage claim 3 had originated in El Paso, Texas. El Paso was on the Mexican border. He didn't have a good feeling about any of this.

"It's Rhoda Rage!" Hearing Rhoda's name shouted from behind, Goodwin turned thinking it would be a relief to see a familiar face, even if it was the annoying Rhoda Rage who had cornered him at the mayor's fundraiser when he had first arrived in Florida. Ten feet away, a group of six buff gay men in tank tops and shorts were pointing to a picture of Rhoda on the cover of *OutClique*, the leading South Florida LGBTQ monthly tourist magazine. They were laughing and shoving each other playfully, happy to be in Fort Lauderdale for a vacation. "Rhoda Rage! That's her name. My friend told me if we make it to Wilton Manors to check out her show. She's epic!"

"Hey." The skinny man in the trench coat was back. He dragged two scuffed-up pieces of mismatched luggage, one red, one gray, behind him. "Help me with these."

Strangely, Goodwin found himself obeying. He reached for the gray one.

"No, no. Take this one." The man led the way to the garage, keeping a faster pace than Goodwin, who trotted ten feet behind pulling the noisy red bag with a busted wheel. Together they put the bags in the back of the SUV. Goodwin, hands shaking, reached for his seatbelt and struggled to get it locked. In the tight confines of the car Goodwin became aware of the stale odor. The man's clothes needed laundering. He needed a shower. Goodwin put his foot on the brake and pressed the ignition. Nothing happened. He tried again. Nothing.

"Everything okay?"

Goodwin didn't answer. He looked down at the gear shift. The car was in neutral. Putting it in park, he stepped on the brake and pressed again. The car started. "Where are we going?"

"Deerfield Beach."

"Yeah, I know, but what address? I'll put it in the GPS."

The man waited a few seconds before answering. Thinking. "Put in the La Quinta. It's the one on Hillsboro Boulevard. Off 95."

"That's where we're going?"

"No. That's *not* where we're going." Goodwin felt like a reprimanded six-year-old who asks too many questions. The man softened. "But close. When we get off at Hillsboro, I'll tell you where to go."

Goodwin headed to the exit and pulled up behind a yellow Mustang with a North Carolina license plate that said, "DA KING." The Mustang's windows were rolled down and deafening rap music blared from the souped-up car. "*So, I run yeah keep me up, creep on me, they speak on me…*" Goodwin's SUV shook. Thump. Thump. Thump. In the rearview mirror Goodwin saw a dirty white van slowly approach behind them. The yellow Mustang wasn't moving. The eardrum piercing rap filled the garage. "*Ladies love my speed, quick to run up trees…*" Goodwin gripped the vibrating steering wheel. The wait to pay was endless. Was this a set up? Would six masked men jump out of the van and gun them down right here in the exit lane of the Hibiscus Garage at Fort Lauderdale International Airport? Goodwin looked over at the stranger sitting next to him. He was peacefully scrolling through text messages on his phone unbothered by the wait or the music. The van behind them let out a long honk that startled Goodwin. The yellow Mustang had disappeared, accelerating up the ramp, music fading quickly. Relieved, Goodwin pulled up and put his debit card into the reader.

"So, where's Tony? I thought I'd be picking him up at the airport."

"Tony?" For a second Goodwin thought the man didn't even know who Tony was. That this was all a mistake. That Tony was back at the airport waiting for Goodwin to pick him up. Then he remembered the man mentioned his name at the baggage claim. The silence in the car returned.

"Tony's already in Deerfield Beach."

"Oh. Why's he in Deerfield Beach?"

The man had said enough. He ignored Goodwin's question and adjusted the air conditioning in the car, making it so cold that Goodwin's hands went numb. Just as Goodwin was about to ask the man his name, the guy's cell phone rang.

"Excuse me. I have to take this."

Goodwin listened intently to the caller on the other end. After a few minutes he cut him off.

"Gotta go. We're almost there."

Just as the man hung up the robotic voice from the GPS announced their next move. "In a quarter mile take the Hillsboro Boulevard exit. Your destination will be on the right."

The La Quinta flew by. For the next five minutes Goodwin listened to the man's monotone directions; turn left, turn right, then right again. Goodwin tried making mental notes of the landmarks they were passing. A Wawa, a bar called The Lucky Lounge, and a place called MegaLo Tires.

"At the light turn left."

The neighborhood was dark and quiet. There were few streetlights. A full moon hung low at the end of the black street and cast a sinister glow over the pavement. Goodwin, eyes darting from side to side, could barely make out the ghostly one-story houses that bordered each side of the deserted street. In the shadows he saw broken fences, discarded toys, a knocked over trash can, a cat pawing at a ripped plastic bag. Somewhere a dog started barking. He knew his life was over; the guy sitting next to him was going to kill him. The canine's barking grew distant as Goodwin drove farther and farther down the blackened asphalt.

"So long, buddy."

"What?" Goodwin stopped the car ready to jump out and run.

"I said, not long buddy, huh? We got here fast. Pull into the driveway."

A single light burned behind the closed curtain of a front window. As Goodwin backed up to turn into the driveway, he saw a red van. Alongside it was Tony's car. His anxiety lessened. Tony wouldn't let anything bad happen to him. Or would he? Goodwin searched for a house number and didn't see one. The boarded-up house next door had an overgrown hibiscus tree covering the spot where a house number might have been.

"Can you pop the back?"

Goodwin felt safer in the car and didn't offer to get out and help. He listened to the man struggling to remove the two suitcases. Goodwin quickly hit "Drive Home" on the GPS, anxious to leave and forget this night had happened.

A hard rap on the car window made Goodwin jump. A dark figure stood outside the door. Tony? At first, Goodwin thought it was, but then saw it was only his passenger waving goodbye. Through the glass he heard a muffled "thanks." Goodwin forced a smile and quickly waved back. As he backed out of the driveway, the door to the house opened spilling a harsh light onto the walkway, casting a shadow of the man that grew longer and longer as he rolled the bags toward the open door. Before driving away, Goodwin took one last look to see if Tony was in the doorway, but it was too late. The door had closed, and the man was gone.

That was his introduction to Stretch Breezy.

ᘓ

Seven months later, alone in the lab, he stared at the kilo of coke on the table. He thought about looking for a new position in another state, California maybe. He was remembering a boyhood trip with his parents to visit a cousin in Santa Barbara, when his phone rang. It was Tony. He didn't want to pick it up, but then he did. The memory of his parents and the magical days traveling the Pacific coast gave him courage. This would be it. He'd tell Tony he was quitting. Moving. Leaving Florida. That he had been thinking of it for a long time. It wasn't anything to do with the, you know…stuff. He just needed a change. A girl had dumped him. He was broken hearted. His mind raced thinking of how to break the news. He'd keep it friendly. "Hi Tony."

He could hear country western music in the background. Then a blender.

"Hey, man. Just checking in. I heard you got all the boxes?"

"Yeah. I have them."

"So? How's it going?"

"I'm. I'm glad you called. I wanted to talk to you."

Tony shouted at someone next to him in the noisy bar. Then he laughed. Goodwin heard a woman's voice then Tony speaking to a bartender. More blender sounds.

"Tony. Hey Tony. Are you there?"

"Yeah, man, I'm here. Sorry. Just calling to check in. How's it going?"

The moment wasn't right. He'd have to tell him face to face. Somewhere public. Somewhere quiet. "I'm just starting. Gotta go." Goodwin hung up the phone. He picked up the box, turned off the lab light, and left the building, promising himself he would call Tony and cut ties tomorrow.

Chapter Fifteen

Rhoda Makes Her Lists

THE turbulent storm had moved up the Florida coast, taking the humidity with it but leaving most of the streets flooded and impassable. Rhoda, safely back home from Drag Bingo, sat silently in her kitchen staring at the refrigerator door. A few weeks ago, Topher, in an effort to lift Rhoda out of one of her periodic "blue funks," had taken some of the multicolored magnetic letters that were scattered across the surface and arranged them to read "SEES THE DAY cleverly misspelling the phrase to disguise the fact that the "I" was missing and Wallie had chewed the "Z" beyond recognition when he was still a puppy.

"It gives it a whole new meaning don't 'cha think?" Topher cheerily declared. "Or not."

A quarter inch of aqua tulle peaked from under the lid of Rhoda's trash can as if contemplating an escape, while the peach tie-dyed leotard, nearing the end of the spin cycle, was soon to have the memory of the evening beat out of it by a brutal dryer and returned to the bottom of the banker's box until the next costume emergency. The Anna May Wong wig, hastily placed on a Styrofoam head on the counter, was being given a thorough airing before its imminent confinement in a zip lock bag shoved to the back of the jewelry drawer. On the table in front of her was the only reminder of the events of the day, the note that had been slipped under her door that morning. For the past hour, Rhoda kept picking it up and putting it down as she roamed from room to room discarding the costume and changing into a soft lavender terrycloth robe and comfy matching slippers. It was almost eleven. She took another sip of her decaffeinated English Breakfast tea and one more time scrolled through her phone to see if somehow she had missed a call from Jimmy. It was her fourth time checking. She gently tapped the phone on the table and stared at nothing. She thought about calling Robin Kradles, but the last vestiges of her energy had evaporated. Listening to her friend explain her way out of a lie, or even worse, continue to lie, would lead Rhoda into saying something she'd regret. Besides, at this hour of the night, Robin was certainly flat on her back at the Island House with her heels pointed to the ceiling. Rhoda warmed her hands on the teacup. Well, maybe she was having a nice time. Hopefully she'd tell Rhoda she had found true love; wouldn't that be nice?

Rhoda looked down at Wallie, sound asleep on her lap. As she lightly stroked the back of his head, the sides of Wallie's lips curled up in a doggy smile, happy that his mommy had returned home from her idiotic night of Drag Bingo. She took another sip of tea and, whispering in Wallie's ear, repeated the three words scratched on the paper.

THE GOLDFISH KNOW

Knows what? And what goldfish? It made no sense. Big Molly was obviously trying to tell her something, something important, but she couldn't figure out what. Rhoda reached for a pad and, without waking Wallie, began writing. Across the top of the page, she wrote "Things I Know." Then she made her list.

1) The note was definitely written by Big Molly, the pad and pencil found in Molly's house confirmed that.

2) The floor lamp in Big Molly's house had been knocked over and stood back up, the ring on the carpet and the dented lampshade both confirmed that.

3) The person that stood the lamp up had three fingers and a thumb on one hand, the left one, the dirty handprint on the inside of the shade confirmed that.

4) The mysterious man she saw going into Sarge's store that morning was the same man that walked into Spencer's Corner that night, Rhoda's own eyes confirmed that.

5) And... most importantly, that very same man had three fingers on his left hand, Benny, Spencer's hot Latino bartender, confirmed that.

All together, these facts meant that Rhoda could place the mysterious man in Big Molly's house before, or shortly after, Big Molly's time of death. But that still didn't tell her who he was or what he was doing there.

Rhoda flipped the page on the pad and on a fresh sheet scrawled across the top "Things I Don't Know...YET."

1)   Who slipped the note under her front door? It couldn't have been Big Molly.

2)   What did the note mean?

3)   Why did Sarge act so nervous when she paid him a visit?

4)   Big Molly's death was confirmed as a heart attack by that pretentious Goodwin, but was it?

5)   Why was Goodwin the first to arrive at Big Molly's house?

6)   Why were there no fingerprints on Molly's doorknob?

7)   Was there a connection between Sarge's store and Big Molly's house?

8)   Jimmy. Ashanti saw him that morning racing down Wilton Drive just before Salvatore D'Angelo got hit by the red van while walking Gooch. Was this somehow connected?

Rhoda underlined Jimmy's name. Twice. Then she drew a circle around it. Jimmy. Where the hell was he? She tapped the pad with the point of the pen, deep in thought. She picked up her cell phone and dialed Jimmy's number. Voicemail again. She hung up and decided to text him. In all caps she wrote:

JIMMY CALL ME

She pressed send. Rhoda stared at the phone waiting for the message to change to "read." When it didn't, Rhoda nodded her head. Something was definitely wrong. Wallie opened his eyes and yawned up at Rhoda, letting her know it was time for bed. She took the two lists and, with Wallie cradled in her arms, walked over to the refrigerator and hung them up using an "S" and the "Y" from Topher's inspirational message. She put

Wallie in the laundry basket on top of the washer so he could watch her as she put the leotard in the dryer. Then she gave his neck a little tickle, picked him up, turned off the light, and headed to the bedroom. Her Marilyn Monroe sleep mask lay ready for her on the bedside table next to a glass of water and a bottle of melatonin. With Wallie still snuggled in one arm, she pulled down the fluffy comforter with the other, kicked off her slippers, and slid into bed still wearing her bathrobe. She placed her cell phone on the table and took a pill. She leaned into the pillows propped up against the headboard and waited for that wonderful feeling of drowsiness to set in. Her eyelids shut as she ran her hand softly across Wallie's back. A burst of thunder filled the room, instantly breaking her languor. Rhoda lifted the sleep mask and glanced down at her phone. She gasped. The message had been changed to "read." Another ferocious thunderclap. The lights flickered. Blackout.

Chapter Sixteen

Play Ball

JIMMY CALL ME

Ignacio grinned as he read Rhoda's text message. He took a deep, slow breath and looked up. Sixty feet away, the batter stood poised, bat held high, waiting anxiously for the pitch. Ignacio gripped the phone tight as the crowd filling the stadium chanted Varga! Varga! Varga! This was his moment. Fingers positioned properly, he drew his right arm back then quickly forward adding a snap of the wrist and a spin. The phone flew fast over the backyard grass heading toward the pitch-black Intracoastal. It landed with a splash somewhere in the middle. Strike One!

Ignacio stared up at the night sky. He loved American baseball. God did he love baseball. He lit a cigarette and slowly walked back to the house.

When Jimmy heard the door to the garage open, his shoulders tensed. His head shot up from under the pillowcase, which he immediately regretted. The slightest movement caused the rope around his wrists to dig deeper into his skin. Heavy footsteps walked toward him. He smelled a cigarette.

"You hungry?"

He couldn't answer. His favorite bandana, the red one he bought twenty years ago during a wild, Fire Island weekend in Cherry Grove, was stuffed in his mouth. He nodded.

"Okay, let me get the menu."

The footsteps withdrew. A door opened. Then closed. The smell of the cigarette lingered. Jimmy, alert in the silence, waited, listening. The door opened. Footsteps. No cigarette.

"Let's see. We got only two choices this late, Hooks chicken or Cuban takeout. Since I'm a nice guy, I'll let you decide. Personally, I like the Cuban. Just sayin'."

Jimmy felt Ignacio's sweaty body leaning oppressively down on him. He ignored the pain and leaned as far back into the chair as he could. He held his breath and turned his head. The cigarette stench and body odor made him gag. He prepared himself for another blow. The one he suffered that morning still resonated across the back of his head. There were two thugs then. Where was the other one? Without warning, the pillowcase flew off. His eyes blinked. Adjusting. The face of his captor stared down at him.

"You must be thirsty. Here." Ignacio removed the bandana and held a bottle of water to Jimmy's lips. Jimmy took long thirsty gulps, water running down his chin. Jimmy studied Ignacio's face. He was hot. Beautiful eyes. Great cheekbones. Suddenly Jimmy didn't care about the stink. Or the rope. Unable to stop staring, Jimmy mumbled, "Cuban."

"Good choice." Manspreading on a step stool five feet away, Ignacio studied the menu. Jimmy's eyes moved across his body, noticing every detail. The guy was built. Thick, muscular thighs, wide shoulders, hairy arms, dark stubble running along the razor-sharp jawline to his chin. And the best part, a huge bulge in his tight jeans. It was already hot in the windowless garage, but this guy made Jimmy sweat. Jimmy fantasied about bartering his freedom for a blow job.

"Let's see… Lechon Asado. I like that. That's shredded pork. Comes with black beans and yellow rice. They put lots of garlic in the pork. Hey, you're not a vegetarian or anything, are you?"

Jimmy shook his head. "I eat everything." He wanted to sound cooperative but felt it came out as flirtatious.

Ignacio did too. "I bet you do." Ignacio punctuated his reply with a wink, causing Jimmy's heart to skip. Maybe bartering was not so crazy after all. He started to ask Ignacio if he'd like a quick massage before dinner, when the door to the garage flew open. The other guy appeared. He was a stud too. Maybe even better. Completely forgetting the danger he was in, he started thinking about a three-way with the two of them.

"Hey. Speed it up. I'm hungry."

"Okay, okay, Martin, I'm just…"

The guy noticed Ignacio had removed the pillowcase. "Iggy!! What the hell did you do?!? Breezy said to wait until he got here."

"What? The guy's got to eat. I wanted to find out what he wanted."

"He'll eat what we give him to eat."

"What if he's a vegetarian?"

Martin rolled his eyes. "You know what the problem with you is, Iggy? The problem with you Iggy is you're TOO FUCKING NICE! Toughen up! Put the pillowcase back on!"

A voice came from behind Martin. "It's okay. Let him be." The new arrival pushed Martin off the two short steps that led down into the garage and walked over to Jimmy. Anticipating another strike to the head, Jimmy tensed up and jerked back. The chair scraped on the cement floor.

"So, my friend, let's you and I have a little talk." The guy circled slowly around Jimmy. When he was directly behind him, he stopped. Ignacio and Martin stared wide-eyed over Jimmy's head, looking like audience members at a low budget horror film. "You two. What are you looking at? Get going before everything closes. Get me something with chicken. Not spicy."

Jimmy watched, amazed how Ignacio and Martin's potent machismo instantly evaporated in the presence of this new person. Clearly, he was the boss. Shoulders hunched, they left the garage arguing about who would drive and fighting over the car keys. Jimmy wished Ignacio had stayed. He'd feel a lot safer. He was different than the other two. He'd given Jimmy water. The garage was once again still, as deathly quiet as it had been during those long, painful hours sitting alone in the chair, ass hurting, feet and ankles cramping. Only this time, without the pillowcase covering his head and the bandana shoved into his mouth, he could see and speak. Jimmy started noticing the details of his surroundings when he heard Ignacio and Martin's footsteps crossing the driveway on the other side of the metal door. Muffled conversation, a burst of laughter, car doors opening, an engine starting then growing distant. They were gone. Should he scream? Maybe a neighbor was walking a dog. What time was it? Suddenly he remembered there was someone standing behind him. Or was there? There was no sound, no rustle or shifting of feet. A drop of warm sweat rolled down Jimmy's neck from behind his right ear and puddled above his trapezius. He tried to shake it off but only caused the salty droplet to move forward and end up resting uncomfortably in his jugular notch.

"Sit still."

Jimmy listened for more but there was only silence. He closed his eyes and waited, expecting the worst. When nothing came, he opened them. They were all going to eat Cuban takeout together. That was a good thing. He would charm them with his personality, tell funny stories, then they'd let him go. That was it. That was his plan. He'd be back home in a few hours. Moving only his eyes he took inventory of his surroundings. Rolls of paper towels stacked on a crooked shelf, a rake, a cracked blue bucket, a busted bird feeder, a rusted charcoal grill with a missing wheel, half a bag of charcoal, and a large brown box. Jimmy squinted. MADE IN CHINA. Above that, in bigger letters, HOLIDAY ORNAMENTS. Jimmy stared at the box thinking about Christmas, his favorite time of year. A small smile crossed his lips. This year he'd throw a party. He'd invite everybody. He'd serve eggnog with lots of rum and tell them all about being tied up in a garage by these hot guys. Robin, Ashanti, Big Molly, Topher, Rhoda. Rhoda! She would be looking for him. He had her wig ready and it was beautiful. His best one yet. He jumped when a hand firmly touched his right shoulder. He could see there were only three fingers and a thumb.

"I'm very sorry about your friend."

Jimmy was confused. What friend? Rhoda? Did something happen to her? Had he been reading Jimmy's mind? "Rhoda?"

"No. She's okay. For now. In fact, I just saw her singing and jokin' around at some gay joint. I was talking about your other friend. The big lady. You know, the one that gave you the note."

"You mean Big Molly?"

"Yeah. Big Molly. Good old Big Molly." Breezy said her name as if remembering a long lost relative that he was fond of.

"Whaaaa—t happened to her?" He was stuttering now. He hadn't stuttered since he was a kid.

"How about I ask you a question first? Then if I like the answer, you can ask me one." Breezy let go of Jimmy's shoulder and walked in front of him. He was holding a gun. "What did the note say?"

Jimmy stared at the gun, unable to speak.

"I said, what did the note say?"

"I-I-I-I dooooooon't know."

"You sure of that?"

"Yes. Yes. She put-put-put-put it in an envelope and sealed it. I wa-wa-wa-watched her do it. She told me to take it to Rhoda's house. She insisted. But she wasn't there. She'd already left. I swear."

"So, you didn't see what the note said?"

"No."

"But you slipped it under her door."

"Yes."

"What about her cell phone?"

"Wha-wha-what cell phone?"

"Molly's. Did she give you her cell phone?"

"No."

Breezy smacked the side of Jimmy's head with the barrel of the gun. Jimmy could feel blood trickle past his ear.

"Come. Come now. She didn't give you her cell phone?"

The blow made Jimmy's stuttering stop. He was angry. "I said no. She only gave me the note."

Breezy didn't say anything. He slowly walked over to the rack of paper towels. He leaned against it resting an elbow on the box from China on the table next to him. He put the gun on top of the box, folded his arms and stared at Jimmy. "You see, I'd like to believe you, but somehow, I can't. After you ran out the back door to deliver your note, I was your friend Molly's next visitor. I asked her for her cell phone, and she said she didn't have it. Now I know she had one. She'd been takin' pictures with it for weeks. So, if she didn't have it, and you say you don't have it, one of you is lying. Which one can it be?"

Jimmy had enough. His heart raced as his anger grew. "I'M NOT LYING!"

Breezy sighed. He picked up the gun and studied it, turning it around in his hands, rubbing Jimmy's blood off the barrel with a nearby rag. He pointed the gun at Jimmy. "Don't ever do that again. Never raise your voice to me."

"I'm sorry."

Breezy continued polishing his gun with the rag, not looking at Jimmy.

"What happened to Molly?"

Breezy smiled a disturbingly sentimental smile. "Your friend wasn't feeling too well. Sorry I couldn't hang around to help. I don't think the ambulance got there in time, though."

"What happened?"

Breezy was about to say something when the door to the garage flew open.

"Dinner!"

Still holding the gun, he looked up at Ignacio and Martin as they came down the steps. "Great! I'm starving."

Chapter Seventeen

Rude Awakening

WITH the Marilyn Monroe sleep mask still covering her eyes, Rhoda groped violently around the items on her nightstand trying to find the phone before it stopped ringing. Jimmy! At last! She knew he'd eventually call. Her hand searched and searched knocking over the bottle of melatonin, the empty water glass, and Deanna Raybourn's new Veronica Speedwell mystery she picked up two weeks ago but couldn't find the time to read. Wallie, burrowed deeply in the folds of the white comforter, jumped out and started running around the bed, barking at the commotion. The ringing stopped.

"Hold on, hold on, Wallie. It's over." Rhoda raised the sleep mask and blinked at the screen. The time was 8:25. She had slept almost an hour longer than she usually did. Every part of her body ached, and she worried she was coming down with a cold. Or, god forbid, Covid. CNN had warned it was making a comeback—and just when she had thrown all her N95s away. She looked at the caller ID. It wasn't Jimmy—no name, just a number. She wondered if it was one of the deleted contacts from her ill-fated Apple tech support call. Arm extended gracefully, she placed the phone back on the nightstand and scooped Wallie up to the pillow and sunk into the bed, tucking the comforter tight around her. "Fifteen more minutes Wallie. Then we'll get up." No sooner had she closed her eyes when the phone started ringing again. "Jesus Christ!" She grabbed it, this time knocking over a tube of moisturizer and a flashlight. The number was the same. Rhoda answered, ready to lash out at an innocent telemarketer. "Hello, did you just call me?"

"Is this Rhoda Rage?"

"Speaking. Who is this?"

"This is Leila Engermann. I'm…"

"Leila! I know you! We met a few years ago at Molly's."

"Yes. Yes. I remember. I was calling you, I hope you don't mind, because Momo, I mean Molly, missed our FaceTime call last night and I'm worried. It's not like her to miss it. I tried calling her all evening and again this morning and there's no answer. Is everything okay?"

Rhoda's stomach clenched. Obviously, no one had gotten in touch with Leila. Guilt shot like a comet across her chest. She should have followed up on that herself. Propped up on one elbow, she struggled with how to break the news. The best way, she decided, was to just say it. "Leila, honey, I'm afraid I have some very bad news. Molly, your Momo, has died."

There was silence on the other end.

Rhoda gave Leila a second to take in her words before continuing. "She was found yesterday morning by Terry, a neighbor who helps Molly with some errands. She was bringing Molly a prescription, and when she got there, Molly was already gone."

Leila, no longer the troubled teenager hustling drinks from old men at Hunters years ago, responded calmly. "How did she die?"

Rhoda, impressed by Leila's maturity, relaxed into the conversation. "Well, they said it was a heart attack."

"They? Who's they?"

"A guy named Goodwin. He's the Deputy Chief Medical Examiner. He was pretty quick to call it." Rhoda immediately regretted the last sentence, but she just couldn't mask her skepticism.

"You don't think it was? A heart attack?"

Rhoda didn't want to sprinkle doubt so early in their talk. Maybe she should let it be. Let Leila have her grief. Rhoda could handle the investigating herself. Besides, Leila would have a lot to do, with estate matters and funeral arrangements. Or maybe Leila could help. Molly had spoken proudly of Leila's accomplishments, a master's degree from Loyola University in Chicago and a successful career in social work. Leila was tough and crafty. By her own will and determination and of course with Molly's love and support, she took herself from being kicked out of home at sixteen by an ultraconservative father in Pembroke Pines to running an inner-city program for LGBTQ youth in Humboldt Park, a rough area of Chicago. If nothing else she could be an astute ear listening to Rhoda's hypotheses and suspicions. "Well…"

"This Goodwin guy, has he done an autopsy?" Leila, practical and unemotional, suddenly became Rhoda's confidante.

"Yes. They did. I mean this Goodwin guy did."

"Then what makes you doubt his conclusion? It sounds like you don't like him."

"Oh, does it show? Well, truth is, I don't really. He's a bit of an upstart."

"Do you think he's hiding something?"

"I can't be sure, but I have my suspicions."

"I see. Where do they have Momo now?"

"She's still at the morgue. I'm sure we can get them to release the body so that you can make funeral arrangements. Unless…"

"Unless what?" Leila was interested in what Rhoda had to say.

"Unless you think there should be a second opinion."

"Do you think there should be one?"

"Couldn't hurt."

Leila's silence on the other end made it clear that she understood Rhoda's doubts were strong enough to warrant suspicions. Molly had always spoken highly about Rhoda, so she knew she wasn't dealing with a silly drag queen. "Many times, Momo told me how smart you were. She'd say, 'Don't mess with Rhoda Rage. She sees things others don't.' I like that. You're a lot like me."

Rhoda felt a strong wave of love wash over her from her new friend. "I can tell."

"So, I trust you completely. I'm happy to request one if you think it's what we should do."

"Are you able to? I mean, do you have the right?" Rhoda felt awful having to say this. She knew Molly had never legally adopted Leila.

Thankfully, Leila wasn't offended. "Not to worry. Two years ago, I had Momo make me her Health Care Surrogate. I also have a copy of her will. So, at the very least, they'll have to listen to me. However, I'm also very familiar with the bureaucratic red tape that gets thrown at you from governmental agencies. So, getting them to think the situation warrants one is another matter altogether. From what I'm hearing from you, all we have are suspicions so I'm not too hopeful."

Rhoda knew Leila was right. At the very least, requesting a second autopsy could be a stall tactic while Rhoda was investigating clues and hunting down evidence. In any case, she was grateful to have had such a meaningful conversation with Leila. Rhoda gave Leila the phone number of the Broward County Medical Examiner's Office and told her to call them and tell them to hold the body until Leila was able to get to Fort Lauderdale. Leila planned on getting the first available flight out of Chicago. Hopefully Rhoda would uncover some new evidence before then. They arranged to meet at Molly's house right after whatever flight she was on landed.

"By the way, who was Molly's doctor?"

"Doctor Margarita Manfredini. Momo loved her." Leila scrolled through her contacts and texted Rhoda the number.

"Thanks Leila. I'll give her a call and tell her we'd like a second opinion. I'll let you know if she thinks it's possible."

"One more thing, Rhoda."

"Yes?"

"I assume Molly's cell phone is still at the house. I'd like to have access to her contacts. I'm sure everyone would want to come to the funeral."

"Funny, I didn't see a cell phone when I was there." Rhoda's mind scanned the table, recalling the *People* magazines, the electric bill, but no cell phone.

"That's strange. She always had it next to her. It was brand new. I gave it to her on her birthday in September when I surprised her with a quick weekend visit. Now I'm glad I did. Have the chance to see her I mean." Leila was quiet. "Anyway, I taught her how to use it. We set her alarms together to remind her to take her medications. Showed her how to take pictures. How to use the zoom feature. She loved that phone."

"I'm certain I didn't see one, Leila, but we can give a good thorough search when you get here."

"Bye Rhoda. I'll call you and let you know what flight I'm on."

The call ended with Rhoda adding one more item to her "Things I Don't Know …YET" list. Molly's cell phone. Was it on the floor under the table? Or in the bedroom? She hadn't really looked around in there. Did the guy with the missing finger have it? And if he did, why did he have it?

Wallie looked at Rhoda and whimpered.

She realized it was almost two hours past his morning walk. The poor thing needed to go badly. "Let's go for a walk!"

Wallie jumped down, ran out of the bedroom and down the hall. Rhoda, pulling up her sweatpants, hopped after him hoping to stop him before he added another scratch mark to her recently painted front door—she really needed to trim his nails but who had the time? She clipped the leash on his purple harness and, after opening the door, checked herself in the mirror before stepping outside. "God, I look a mess!"

Wallie, desperate to do his business, yanked the leash out of Rhoda's hand and bolted. He raced down the walkway and immediately squatted, nose pointed to the sky, tears of relief filling his tiny eyes. Rhoda trotted up behind him and reached down for the end of the leash. However, before she had her hand on it, Wallie spotted the mooching iguana that had been freeloading in Rhoda's parking spot the day before and went on a frenzied pursuit of the reptilian intruder, barking and chasing him across the asphalt clear to the other side of the lot. The iguana, fearing for his life, shot up a tree and stared down at the menacing toy fox terrier from the safety of a branch ten feet off the ground. Wallie jumped and barked wildly as Rhoda caught up.

"Whoa, Wallie, easy boy! It's only an—"

Rhoda stopped. Her face frozen in shock. There, parked in the space directly under the tree, and only thirty feet from her front door, was Jimmy's beat up 1987 Nissan Sentra with the missing rear bumper and the taped-on side mirror.

Chapter Eighteen

Stinky Business

RHODA watched transfixed as Phil McConnell slowly circled around Jimmy's car, peering inside from every angle. He was about to open the driver's side door when Rhoda stopped him. "Ah, ah, ah. Not without these you don't. Here." Rhoda held out the pair of latex gloves she had retrieved from her condo after calling Phil and asking him to meet her right away in her parking lot in Palm Aire. She had felt awful when he told her it was his day off and that she was pulling him away from painting his boy's bedroom.

"This had better be important."

"Oh, it is Phil. Believe me."

When he showed up twenty minutes later, hair a mess, wearing workout shorts and a paint-splattered old baby blue dress shirt unbuttoned low enough to hint at the well-toned pecs beneath, he was surprised as she was to see Jimmy's car. With Phil looking like Bradley Cooper in *The Hangover*, Rhoda found it hard concentrating on the dilapidated vehicle.

Sweating in the unusual early morning Florida heat, she fanned herself with Molly's mysterious goldfish letter that she had grabbed off her kitchen table when she went back for the gloves. She planned on showing it to Phil after they finished inspecting the car.

Phil put the gloves on, opened the door, sat in the driver's seat, and poked around. He looked in the glove compartment. Nothing of interest. A bunch of crumpled receipts. Two melted Snickers bars. A box of condoms. The car smelled like Jimmy. It needed a bath.

Wallie, who had long forgotten the iguana, shifted his attention to the car's tires, raising his leg several times to add his scent to the already odiferous vehicle. Mid-tinkle, he suddenly began barking and bolted to the rear of the car. Rhoda grabbed Phil's arm, pulling him from the driver's seat, racing down the side of the Sentra where they found Wallie, tiny front legs propped up on the back of the car, sniffing and yapping uncontrollably along the edges of the closed trunk. Rhoda and Phil stared as Wallie grew more and more agitated with every inhale. Their heads turned toward each other. Neither one spoke. Rhoda was caught off guard by the frightened look in Phil's eyes.

"Should we look inside, Phil?"

"We have to. Wait here."

Phil returned to the driver's side, felt around under the dash, then popped the trunk. When he reappeared, he noticed Rhoda had taken a few steps back and Wallie was now quivering at her side. Cautiously, Phil approached the rear of the car and ever so slowly raised the hatch as if to postpone the discovery of whatever gruesome thing might lie inside, the irritating squeak from the worn trunk hinges adding to the suspense. Rhoda expected Bela Lugosi to pop up and say "Good evening..." She stepped back even further, covering her eyes and turning her head as Phil leaned in.

"Oh my God! The smell!"

Rhoda's heart stopped. She moved her hand over her mouth muffling a scream. "Phil, is it Jimmy?"

"No. Wendy."

Rhoda dropped her hand. Wendy? How did Ashanti's on-again off-again girlfriend end up in the trunk of Jimmy's car? Rhoda closed her eyes, mumbled "dear God" and crossed herself. She baby-stepped over to the trunk and grabbed Phil's hand. Fingers locked, standing side by side, little Wallie fully extended on his hind legs desperately trying to see inside, they looked down and stared blankly at a Wendy's half-eaten cheeseburger, the paper wrapper lying next to it covered in ants. Fossilized french fries were scattered across the bed of the trunk.

"Good thing you made me put these on!" Phil, held up the rancid burger with two fingers, keeping it far away from his nose, and started digging around inside the trunk with his free hand.

"Gimme that!" Rhoda grabbed the burger and pitched it over the hedge. "Some pelican will enjoy a good breakfast."

Together they rummaged around in Jimmy's trunk, brushing french fries out of the way. The trunk was a disaster. Wig supplies, cans of hair spray, Styrofoam heads, plastic bags, and a box of hangers were tossed helter-skelter inside. Rhoda was grateful her wig was not among the detritus. If it were, she'd never put it on her head. Side by side, they leaned into the trunk deeper and deeper, so absorbed in their search they did not hear the tiny footsteps that approached them softly from behind. Rhoda froze mid-search when she felt a firm poke on her ass. She whispered "Phil." He whispered back "What?" Rhoda held a finger up signaling to be quiet. "I think someone's behind us." She picked up a plastic hanger. She quietly slid one toward Phil realizing he wasn't armed.

Hangers in hand, they slowly turned around coming face to face with a little girl wearing an *Encanto* T-shirt and striped, pink shorts. She was holding a fluffy cat that was almost as big as she was. The girl petted the cat's long, ginger fur as it slept peacefully in her arms. "Are you looking for the man?"

Rhoda recognized the girl. She lived with her mother a few doors down, but Rhoda didn't know her name. "Why yes. Yes, we are. We're looking for our friend. His name is Jimmy. Have you seen him?"

"Uh-huh."

"Well, can you tell us where he is?"

The girl stared stone-faced at Rhoda as she stroked the kitty.

Phil immediately realized that dealing with a child, especially a precocious one, was not a skill in Rhoda's wheelhouse and he jumped in to help. He began by giving the girl a big toothy smile. "You're a very pretty little girl. What's your name, honey?"

"Myrtle."

Rhoda, thinking what kind of mother would name their kid Myrtle, started to laugh.

Phil shot her a look. He turned back to the girl with an even bigger smile. "Myrtle! What a lovely name! Tell me Myrtle, when did you see our friend?"

"Yesterday. I'm five years old."

"Five! You're quite the young lady! Now then, tell us what happened when you saw our friend?"

"This is my cat Obi. Do you want to pet him?"

This was going to be slow business. Rhoda considered taking a shower and making coffee while Phil gathered the information but decided to stick it out.

"No honey. We need to find our friend. Tell me Myrtle, when you saw our friend yesterday, what was he doing?"

"If you pet my cat, I'll tell you."

Rhoda's eyebrows shot up. Blackmailed by a five-year-old. Rhoda hated cats. She found them sneaky and disinterested in their owners. Dogs were smart. You could train a dog. And dogs gave you a lot of attention, something that Rhoda craved. She looked around for Wallie and panicked when she didn't see him. Rhoda bent down to look under the car and found him hunched next to a rear tire quietly growling. He felt the same way about precocious little girls and their kitties.

Prepared to go the extra mile to find Jimmy and finding no other way to extract the needed information, Rhoda stood up, took a deep breath and extended her hand to pet the cat. But before fingers felt fur, Phil, sensing Rhoda's dilemma, saved the day.

"Here Myrtle. I'll pet him."

The little girl gazed lovingly up at Phil, admiring his handsome features and his big blue eyes. Phil smiled at Myrtle and stroked the cat's back. Obi, contented, looked at Phil and purred.

Rhoda, frustrated and craving caffeine, looked at Myrtle and barked. "Okay, Myrtle. Back to our friend. When you saw our friend, what was he doing?"

The little girl, eyes locked on Phil, giggled. "He was getting in a big red truck. There was a swimming pool on it! I love to swim!"

"I bet you do, honey. Was our friend getting in the big red truck alone?"

The girl's expression changed, becoming dark and somber. She frowned and directed her reply straight into Rhoda's eyes. "No. There were two big men with him. They were mean. They hit him. I told my mother, but she didn't believe me. She says I make things up. But I don't."

"I'm sure you don't, honey. You're a very smart little girl."

Rhoda, making progress, pressed on. "Is there anything else you can tell us?"

Myrtle looked back at Phil who was still petting Obi. "Are you a Prince?"

Rhoda rolled her eyes. Phil, however, was flattered by the compliment, even if it was coming from a five-year-old. "No sweetie. I'm a Police Officer."

"Oh."

Rhoda needed to speed up their interrogation. Now that they knew Jimmy was abducted by "two big men" in a "big red truck," they had to find him fast. She repeated her question but with a rougher edge. "Myrtle, was there anything else you saw?"

Myrtle looked at Rhoda dismissively. She ran her five-year-old eyes up and down Rhoda's body deciding whether she was worthy of a reply. "Are you a witch?"

A witch! The girl's rudeness was shocking. Rhoda knew she didn't look her best, having had no time to comb her hair or put on makeup, but she didn't think she looked that bad. Clearly the girl's mother hadn't taught little Myrtle any manners. How dare the little impudent…

Phil, embarrassed for Rhoda, once again came to her rescue. "No, Myrtle. My friend isn't a witch. She's a very nice lady who is very good to people."

Myrtle, thinking herself a better judge of character than Phil, was having none of it. "Well, I still think she's a witch."

And with that, five-year-old Myrtle turned on her heels and walked away with Obi, still fast asleep in her arms. Phil and Rhoda stood there, slacked-jawed, in an awkward silence. Wallie inched out from under the car as Phil broke the ice. "Well Rhoda, it looks like your suspicions were correct. Something has happened to Jimmy. Something really bad."

Rhoda, deep in her own thoughts, wasn't listening. She was thinking about something Phil had said yesterday morning when she was stuck in traffic on Wilton Drive. "Phil, didn't you tell me that Salvatore D'Angelo was knocked down by a red van when he was walking Gooch?"

"That's right. He said it was red."

Rhoda, pacing up and down in the parking lot, reconstructed Tuesday morning's timeline in her head. Phil and Wallie watched intently as Rhoda mumbled to herself, occasionally pointing a finger in the air to emphasize a thought or stopping in her tracks now and then when clarity struck. "Phil, I think I figured it out."

"You have?"

Rhoda ran her hands through her hair and prepared to deliver a performance to her audience of two. "Here's what I think happened. Ashanti saw Jimmy's car racing down Wilton Drive shortly before eight. Seconds later a red van struck Mr. D'Angelo sending him flying to the curb. Jimmy, on his way to my house to deliver this message written by Big Molly…" Rhoda waved the paper high in the air for dramatic affect. It caught Phil's attention.

"Message?" Phil tried to grab it from her hand, but Rhoda pulled it away.

"I'll get to that in a minute. Jimmy was being followed by the red van. Are you with me?"

Phil was still staring at the paper, curious as to what is said. Rhoda held it behind her back.

"Pay attention. Once Jimmy got here, he had just enough time to run over to my door and slip it under. Unfortunately, he didn't have enough time to get back in his car and skedaddle. And sweet little five-year-old Myrtle witnessed the whole thing. Jimmy being hit over the head, put in the van, and driven away."

"But Rhoda, if Jimmy knew he was being followed, why did he park over here and not right in front of your door?" They looked plaintively at the back of Jimmy's car. Rhoda didn't have an answer.

"Maybe he didn't know he was being followed?"

Rhoda heard a sound coming from above her. She looked up. The iguana was making a slow descent to a tree branch with a better view.

"Of course! The iguana."

Phil didn't understand. "The iguana?"

"The iguana was sleeping in my parking space. Jimmy probably saw it and parked over here."

"Oh." Phil nodded. "One more thing, Myrtle didn't say he was hit over the head."

"Okay, okay, but she did say he was hit. Will ya stop interrupting?"

"Sorry."

Phil watched Rhoda as she tapped the roof of the car, thinking, thinking, thinking. Where did they take Jimmy? Was he hurt badly? She looked around for Myrtle, but she had disappeared inside her house with her cat. Just as well. While Rhoda would have liked to extract a bit more information out of Myrtle, she didn't want to risk another insult. Instead, she held out the note.

"Okay, now you can read it."

Phil studied the paper. "THE GOLDFISH KNOW" He looked quizzically at Rhoda. "This is what Jimmy was racing to your house to give you?"

"Yes."

"What does it mean?"

"Your guess is as good as mine. But I'm certain that it has something to do with Big Molly's death and why Jimmy was nabbed in my parking lot."

Phil turned the note over and looked at the back. He shook his head. "You think so?"

"I know so." They stood in silence before Rhoda continued. "I didn't mention the note to you yesterday, Phil. I wanted to be sure there was a connection."

"So, what do we do now, Rho?"

As good as Phil was at maintaining the peace in Wilton Manors, he was clearly no sleuth. Rhoda would have to do all the heavy lifting herself. "I say we have a chat with Mr. D'Angelo. Maybe he can recall something about the red van or at least confirm there was a swimming pool on it. Anything would help."

"Good idea, Rho. Uh… but can I run home and rinse out my paint brushes?"

"Sure Phil. Let's meet up at Sal's in an hour. No, make it eleven. I could use a cup of coffee and a shower. Oh, and keep that shirt unbuttoned. Maybe Sal will be a bit more forthcoming." Rhoda turned and headed back to her house, Wallie trotting behind. Phil, confused, looked down at his sweat dotted pecs wondering what in the world did she mean?

Chapter Nineteen

Hop to It

JIMMY'S eyes slowly focused on the thin, bright line of sunlight coming from under the garage door. The unrelenting deluge that had beaten mercilessly upon the tar roof and turned the gutters into Niagara Falls was finally over. Gone were the continuous claps of thunder and hair-raising sparks of lightning. The wake of the storm brought a cloudless dawn and unbearable humidity that slipped stealthily under the metal door turning the space into a deathly sauna. Breathing was a chore. Before daybreak, when the explosive barrage had finally subsided, Jimmy had dozed off for just a few minutes but was woken abruptly, not by the light nor the rising heat, but by the sound of a garbage truck turning the corner and heading slowly down the block. He listened, anticipating a miracle, as the muffled shouts of the two trash collectors grew closer and closer joining the chorus of banging cans and the diesel motor's hum. He raised his chin to the ceiling like a wolf howling at the moon quickly realizing screaming was impossible. Martin, on Breezy's command, had stuffed Jimmy's red Cherry Grove bandanna back in his mouth holding it in place with three-inch-wide duct tape. When he moved his head in any direction except up, the tape pulled painfully at the hair on the back of his neck. Thankfully they had left the pillowcase off. Aside from a brief bathroom break after the garlicky pork and beans, Jimmy had been sitting in the folding chair for close to twenty-four hours. His neck was stiff, his wrists ached, his feet were numb and swollen.

He listened with diminishing hopefulness as the banter of the trash collectors faded away, leaving behind a desolate stillness and a faint aroma of empty trash cans. The house was quiet. He wondered if his captors were still asleep. Or if they had left. He leaned forward in the chair as far as the restraints would allow and listened for sounds, running water, a television perhaps. Nothing. The chair, in the center of the space, was too far away from the door. He knew from his quick walk to the bathroom hours ago that the kitchen was directly behind the door. Jimmy replayed the brief moments of freedom remembering every detail, every turn, simultaneously consoling himself and blaming himself for his inability to escape. Past the kitchen was the dining area with a large glass table. The table was littered with the remnants of the Cuban take out meal and all the chairs had been pushed back as if the occupants had fled the room in a hurry. Beyond the dining area he had glimpsed the back of a sofa—was someone lying on it?—and a large screen TV mounted on the far wall which surprisingly showed a nature documentary. The sound was off. Yes. It was like walking through a dream. The placid whale swimming across the screen had given him a second of relief from his constant state of anxiety but was quickly broken by Martin's hand shoving him hard into the bathroom. "Make it fast."

Sitting on the toilet, he had studied his surroundings. There was no window. He had flushed—did he?—and quietly stood, turned the faucet on full, and began searching knowing he had only seconds to find something that could help him. His captors, however, must have anticipated this and had stripped the room of any object that might have assisted him. The medicine cabinet was completely empty. No pills to throw on the floor behind him as he ran down the hall. No cuticle scissor, nail clipper, or file. The vanity drawer contained a strand of wavy black hair, mold in the corners, and nothing else. No towels on the towel bars to throw over someone's head and no toothbrush to jab someone in the gut. The only things left were half a roll of one-ply toilet paper and a slimy bar of Dial soap on a ledge in the shower. The mucky yellow bar had a similar black hair attached to it. He remembered standing at the sink pulling the wet toilet paper from between his fingers and seeing the frosted-glass shower door reflected in the medicine cabinet mirror and thinking of a farfetched plan that now, sitting in the soupy, fetid air of the garage, he wished he had tried. He'd break the glass with his elbow, grab a sizable shard then hide behind the door, quietly unlock it and when Martin walked in, he'd slice his throat from behind. But then the sudden rap on the bathroom door had broken the fantasy.

"Hurry up in there."

The moments after that were hazy. He didn't remember opening the door, returning to the garage, getting retied in the chair. Now, hours later, alone and broken, his body stiff and swollen, he began to sob thinking this sliver of light, this bright iridescent line, would be the last sunshine he'd ever see. Uncontrollably he twisted and turned in the chair violently fighting the constraints that held him, determined to win. With each sob he bounced higher, a quarter inch, then a half inch off the floor landing harder in the seat each time, the pain telling him to fight, push. Finally exhausted, with nothing left, he sat staring at the yellow line which had magically turned into thousands of lines through the prism of his tear-filled eyes. A sad, simple smile came across his mouth. He thought of his mother and how much he loved her. His head slumped in defeat and a single teardrop fell to the floor between his knees. Suddenly, as if a benevolent god was pointing the way, his face softened. He noticed that the force of his spasmodic movements had carried him three or four inches from his original spot.

It occurred to him that if he hopped up and down in the chair, just a tiny bit, he could move the chair closer to the door. The thought of escape returned but this time filled with a realistic possibility of success. Ignoring the pain, he turned his head as far as he could in each direction, looking to see if there was anything to help set him free. If he spotted scissors, a knife, a paint scraper, he'd move the chair in that direction. The metal worktable to his right had sharp edges. He could position himself with his back to one of the legs and slowly move his hands along the sharp edge to saw through the rope. He gave a hop. The chair moved a half inch. This would work. He inhaled deeply, tensed every muscle in his body and prepared to hop again. Then the door opened.

"Well, good morning. Did you have a nice night?"

Jimmy stared at Breezy grinning in the doorway hoping that he wouldn't notice the chair had slightly moved. The fear of being caught trying to escape began to overwhelm him. Suddenly he was freezing. He started to shiver. Breezy slowly crossed toward him and stopped when he was directly in front of the chair. He looked down at the floor and tilted his head to one side. Then he moved behind Jimmy and ripped the duct tape off his neck in one swift pull.

"If you start to scream the gag goes back on. Understand?"

Jimmy pushed the bandana out with his tongue and nodded his head. He wouldn't utter a peep. The bandana fell to his lap. Breezy grabbed it and threw it to the floor. If the gag stayed off that was a good thing. One small victory. Now if he could only free his hands.

"I told the boys to bring you some coffee and a bagel. I have to take care of a few things, but when I get back, I'll figure out what I'm going to do with you." Breezy walked to the door and opened it. Before he left, he turned around and looked at Jimmy. "I hate to see this thing end badly, you know, like it did for your big lady friend. She shouldn't have given you that note. No sir. But, since she did, my options are kind of limited at this point. You understand." Breezy left the garage, closing the door behind him. Jimmy started to cry. They were going to kill him. He was sure of it. Breezy's words weren't a threat, they were a statement of fact. The tears ran down his face. Mucus filled his nose and throat. He mumbled "please, please" but there was no one to hear him. Crestfallen, he hung his head and sobbed.

"Good morning! Rise and shine!"

Jimmy looked up. Ignacio walked down the two steps with a cup of coffee and a bagel. His hair was still wet from the shower, and he had on a tight white t-shirt that emphasized his wide shoulders and the solid abs that lay underneath. "I hope you like milk and sugar because that's how I made it."

Jimmy had no stomach for food. He was too upset thinking about his life ending in the garage. He thought once more of his mother. Who would look after her? Ignacio noticed the puddle of tears in Jimmy's eyes. "What's the matter with you?"

He pulled up a chair and held the coffee to Jimmy's lips. As their eyes locked Jimmy took a sip. There was a pleasant gentleness that contrasted with his big hands and hard muscular forearms. Jimmy had thought this the night before when Ignacio spoon-fed him the rice and beans, taking extra care not to get any on Jimmy's lap. He even wiped his mouth with a napkin when he was finished. Ignacio broke off a piece of the bagel and held it up. Jimmy opened his mouth and as the bagel approached his lips his shoulders slumped. "You're going to kill me."

Ignacio pulled the bagel away, surprised at the comment. "What? Who told you that?"

"The other guy."

"He said that?"

"No. Well, he implied it."

This was obviously news to Ignacio. Ignacio shook his head. "Nah. Don't worry. Everything will be just fine. Here, have some bagel. I'm sorry we don't have anything else in the fridge."

The door opened again. This time it was Martin. "Iggy, come on. Shove the fucking bagel in his mouth and leave him alone. Breezy's coming back and he wants us to go with him to the store."

"To The Moon?"

"Yeah. So, hurry up."

Jimmy caught the name of Sarge's store and wondered why they were going there. To kill Sarge next? What the hell was going on?

"Okay, okay, give me a minute. I'll be right in." Ignacio tapped Jimmy's knee and gave him a reassuring wink. He held up the bagel. "Here. Eat something." Suddenly, Jimmy felt he had a protector, someone on his side.

Jimmy, not wanting Ignacio to leave, started eating the bagel. When Martin closed the door behind him, Jimmy took his chance. "Can you help me?"

Ignacio did not answer. He kept breaking off pieces of the bagel and holding them up to Jimmy's mouth. In between swallows Jimmy asked again. "Can you help me? Please."

Instead of answering, Ignacio told Jimmy a story. "You know, back in Slovakia, I have a cousin who's like you. I don't mind, but Martin, he doesn't like our cousin. He calls him a "ritopich" which is Slovak for shitass. Here, in this country, you say the word faggot. Same thing. But like I said, I don't mind. When we get back, I'll bring you some lunch." Without looking at Jimmy, he stood up, brushed bagel crumbs from his pants, and left the garage.

Jimmy realized Ignacio was only being nice to him because he liked his cousin back in Slovakia. He'd never help

Jimmy escape. Loud music started playing from somewhere in the house. He heard the brothers arguing. The music changed from heavy metal to rock. Then back again. More fighting. Adrenaline shot through Jimmy's body. He only had a little bit of time before Breezy returned. The music would be a good cover as Jimmy put his plan into action. He'd have to work fast. He inhaled deeply, tensed every muscle in his body, and started hopping toward the table.

Chapter Twenty

La Cage aux Sal

RHODA, freshly showered, caffeinated, and wearing a flattering lemon yellow tunic blouse cinched at the waist by a cerulean scarf over beige stretch jersey capri pants, and Phil, still in the baby blue paint splattered unbuttoned shirt and workout shorts per Rhoda's instructions, headed up the walkway to the beautifully landscaped ranch house of Salvatore D'Angelo on NE 20th Street in Wilton Manors. As Wallie sniffed the boxwoods lining the pavers, Rhoda began worrying that this visit would be a complete waste of precious time. Jimmy, her best friend and wig designer par excellence, was in danger and they needed to find him—fast! Besides, Salvatore D'Angelo had already told Phil that all he remembered was that the van was red, a fact confirmed by little Myrtle. Okay, now what? Why were they even here? She hesitated before ringing the doorbell. Maybe they should turn around and focus their attention someplace else. But where? They had no other leads. Before Rhoda could express her doubts, Phil leaned in and pressed the button. Too late now, Rhoda thought. The doorbell began its musical chime. Rhoda recognized the tune but didn't recall the name of the song. It was a show tune, that she was sure of. Was it from *Cats* or *Cabaret*? Or maybe *Carousel*? She rang the doorbell a second time, hoping that if she heard the tune again, she'd remember. As Rhoda waited for the tune to play out, Wallie sniffed along the bottom of the door, tail wagging happily. Phil, hands in the pockets of his Champion shorts, stood quietly to the side staring at a plaster statue of David that stood next to the front door on a stone pedestal. The statue was ornamented with a set of cheap pearls and a rainbow scarf tied around its privates. Phil, not knowing what to make of the statue or the added accoutrements, was oblivious to the bell's tune. No need asking him, she thought. He wouldn't know any show tunes.

Rhoda hummed along as the doorbell played the sixteen notes. She still couldn't place it. Before it finished, however, a booming baritone called out from inside.

"Hold on! I'm coooooooooming!" The door flew open and there stood Salvatore D'Angelo, possibly the gayest man in all of Wilton Manors. He was wearing a bright floral silk shirt in shades of pink and turquoise and a pair of crisp white shorts with a yellow belt. On his feet, a pair of well-worn Gucci loafers with no socks. His thinning hair, badly dyed a bright orange, was cut in a style suitable for a twenty-year-old pop star, Justin Bieber perhaps, but not a seventy-two-year-old Florida retiree. His right arm was in a navy-blue sling from yesterday's traffic accident. Gooch, his devoted Pomeranian, jumped up and down, excited to have visitors, one of which happened to be another dog. Salvatore D'Angelo's jaw dropped when he saw Rhoda.

"RHODA RAGE! Oh my God! To what do I owe the honor of this visit? Come in, come in!" Salvatore D'Angelo was so impressed to have the famous Rhoda Rage cross his threshold that he began shutting the door in Phil's face. "Oh! Excuse me! Officer Phil. Good seeing you again. I didn't recognize you out of uniform. My, that shirt is a pretty shade of blue. Is it pima cotton?" Salvatore decided to find out for himself and slid two fingers into Phil's unbuttoned shirt, evaluating the material but also brushing them against Phil's well-developed pectoral muscles. "My, my, such strong fabric. Come in, come in. And thank you for your help yesterday. It was very sweet of you to hold my hand while we waited for the ambulance together."

Salvatore batted his hazel eyes at Phil while Gooch let out a guttural "woof" as if in agreement.

"Let's all sit in the living room, shall we? It's so very nice and cheery." He led his guests down a mirrored hallway into an enormous, all-white living room with large sliding doors that led out to a sparkling, kidney-shaped pool. The furniture was pristine but dated, as if he had a decorator do it thirty years ago and never changed a thing. Salvatore, proud of his home and loving the opportunity to show it off, stood there with his hands clasped in front of him, allowing Rhoda and Phil to take it all in. As they stood there, blinded by all the whiteness; white sofas, white carpet, white tables, and white draperies, Salvatore delicately tiptoed over to a Lalique vase sitting on a white end table and moved it ever so slightly to the right. "Please forgive the mess! The housekeeper comes tomorrow."

Rhoda looked around. Aside from this week's *TV Guide* lying on the floor next to a chair, nothing was out of place. "Sal, if I may call you Sal…" Rhoda began.

"Oh, please do, please do. And I shall call you Rhoda. There! We are now good friends!"

"Yes. Sal, that tune the doorbell plays, I know I know it, but for the life of me I can't remember the name. What is it?"

Salvatore gave Rhoda a tight-lipped smile, his eyes twinkling in sheer pleasure. He had stumped the great Rhoda Rage! "Why it's Jerry Herman of course! 'If He Walked Into My Life Today.' From *Mame*!" To punctuate his remark, his left arm swept across the vast expanse of the living room, a la Mame Dennis, causing Rhoda to notice all the Jerry Herman posters from every Jerry Herman musical adorning the walls. They were quite large and spectacularly hung in pure white lacquered frames. They must have cost a fortune. Clearly Salvatore D'Angelo was a fan.

"Oh, you like Jerry Herman?" Rhoda asked.

"Like him? I adore him! Not only was he the greatest musical comedy composer *and* lyricist that ever lived, he was also a fabulous decorator." Salvatore winked at Rhoda and pointed to an old issue of *Architectural Digest* that was placed dead center on the white and chrome Parsons coffee table. Rhoda leaned down to read the cover: *Jerry Herman in Bel Air.* "That's his home in California. Page 97. Well, one of his homes. He's had thirty-eight. Even a few here in Florida. Let's see… Miami, Coral Gables, Key West. In fact, you're standing in a replica of his Miami living room."

"Oh" was all Rhoda had to offer. The room was far too sterile for her taste.

Sal thought for a second before adding, "Well, as close as I could get. Some things are a bit different, like that armoire." He pointed to a cabinet that was slightly smaller than a two-car garage. Rhoda wondered how the hell they got it through the door. "But the room is a very close replica. It's an homage, if you will. A photographer for *SunSentinel* wanted to photograph it for a Sunday feature." On this, Salvatore's eyes looked down. He suddenly became solemn. "It's such a pity he died."

"Who?" Rhoda asked. "The photographer?"

"No! Jerry Herman! I was sure he had a few more shows left in him. Tsk. Tsk."

A pity he died? Wasn't he like 101 years old? Rhoda remembered reading about it in the paper. She nodded in agreement. "Yes, such a pity," Rhoda said. And then, just because, she shook her head and added "So young."

Salvatore nodded in agreement. "Yes indeed. So young. I don't suppose you perform any of his songs in your nightclub act, Miss Rage?" Salvatore D'Angelo was definitely old-school, calling Rhoda's campy drag show a nightclub act.

"Yes. In fact, I did a version of 'So Long Dearie' where I changed the lyrics." Rhoda started singing, *"Wave your big fat schlong because it too long dearie, you ain't gonna schtup me on the floor."* Rhoda started laughing hysterically at her own cleverness. "It was a hoot, Sal. A real hoot. It was all about meeting a guy with a big, fat, long—"

Salvatore, shocked, interrupted Rhoda. He was clearly bothered by the vulgarization of one of Jerry Herman's most beloved songs. "Change the lyrics? Why on earth would you do that?"

Rhoda, realizing her faux pas, tried to cover. "Oh, you know what, my mistake Sal, it wasn't 'So Long Dearie,' it was a tune by Kander and Ebb. That's right, Kander and Ebb."

"Ugh. Kander and Ebb. Such horrible songwriters. Good thing you changed the lyrics." Salvatore squeezed Rhoda's arm and led them to the sofa. Rhoda and Phil began to sit but Gooch jumped up and sat down first. "Not there! That's Gooch's spot."

Rhoda and Phil politely made room for Gooch, sitting down on either side of the shaggy pup. Rhoda started thinking that dealing with five-year-old Myrtle and her cat Obi was a breeze compared to Sal and Gooch. She looked around for her sweet little Wallie. Where did he go? She turned her head in every direction and suddenly, when she spotted him, she froze, her eyes widening in horror. He was on the other side of the room, directly behind Sal, squatting on the carpet. She couldn't stop it. Out it came. A steady, golden stream soaking into the snow-white silk pile. Sal, oblivious to what was happening behind him, noticed Rhoda's open mouth.

"Are you all right, Rhoda? Would you like a cool beverage? Some lemonade?"

"Uh, no thank you, Sal."

"And you, Officer? A cold Bud perhaps? I also have Coors Light."

"No, thank you Sal. I'm good."

Wallie, finished with his business, walked over to the sofa, jumped up, and fell asleep on Rhoda's lap as Gooch began sniffing Wallie's backside.

"Uh… We can't stay long Sal. Phil and I just wanted to pop over for a few minutes and ask you if you recalled anything else about the accident yesterday. Specifically, about the van that hit you. Phil said you told him it was red, is that correct?"

"Yes, it was! A bright red! The color of Dolly's dress when she descends the staircase at Harmonia Gardens! A lovely shade!"

Rhoda looked at Phil and smiled. Phil, however, looked confused. "Dolly? Who's Dolly?"

Rhoda patted his knee letting him know she'd handle it. "Anything else Sal?"

"Aside from my badly bruised right elbow that now leaves me unable to play?"

"Play what?" Rhoda asked. "Tennis?"

"Tennis! Dear god no! The piano!" Salvatore's left arm once again dramatically swept the room ending at the archway that led to an all-white den with a white baby grand piano. On top of the piano, in an expensive silver frame from Tiffany's, was a large black and white photo of Sal and Jerry Herman taken at the opening night of *La Cage aux Folles* at the Kravis Center in Palm Beach many moons ago. "I *must* rehearse! I have a holiday show coming up in December at The Sunshine Cathedral. A musical tribute to Jerry Herman. I'm calling it *Making Merry with Jerry*! What do you think? Clever, no? We're raising money for SAGE."

"Yes. Very clever."

"Sage? Who's Sage?" Phil wasn't following any of this.

"You know Rhoda, everyone is dying to be in the show and do a number. However, I'm very picky about who I let perform. But... if you would like to do something... I'm sure I could squeeze you —"

This time it was Rhoda who cut Sal off. "Gee, Sal that's awfully nice of you but my December is chock-full. I don't even have time to blow my nose." This was a lie, but Rhoda could not imagine singing a Jerry Herman song in a show produced and directed by Salvatore D'Angelo.

"Another time then, perhaps?"

"Sure, Sal, sure. Now, back to the red van…"

"Oh, yes. That. Well, if you really want to find out more, you should ask the Merlots. They saw everything."

"The Merlots?" Now it was Rhoda's turn to look confused.

"Ethel and Vivian Merlot. The two gals that took care of Gooch while they carted me off to Holy Cross. Such wonderful gals. When they got married a few years ago, they changed their last name to their favorite wine! Isn't that wonderful! Of course, if I ever got married, I'd have to change mine to Gin-Rickey. I just loooove Gin Rickeys. Don't you? Anyway, you should talk to them. As I said, they saw everything."

Finally, a lead! "Where can we find them? The Merlots?"

"Why, right next door! They're my neighbors. They're on the other side of the hedges. Come with me."

A blast of steamy hot Florida air hit Rhoda and Phil in the face as Sal slid open the patio door. Wallie and Gooch, having sniffed each other out on the sofa, now started running around the pool playing a doggy version of tag. Sal led his guests to the long line of manicured clusia hedges along one side of his property. There was a space between two of the hedges that Sal stuck his head through.

"Yoo-hoo!!! Ladies!! We have company! The famous Rhoda Rage is here!!"

Rhoda felt uncomfortable that Sal was making such a big deal of her visit. She was there for one purpose only, to get information to help find Jimmy and to find out what may have actually happened to Big Molly. She wasn't there to get her ego stroked.

Sal took a step back as the hedges parted further. The robust figure of Vivian Merlot appeared followed by the slender figure of her wife, Ethel. They wore matching lavender Polo shirts and sipped iced tea out of matching Starbuck rainbow tumblers. "Hiya Sal! What's up? How's your arm?"

Sal played the martyr to perfection. "Oh, it's killing me. I was just telling Rhoda, you know Rhoda don't you, and Officer Phil, that I can't play the piano and I have to get ready for my show! You are coming, aren't you?"

"We wouldn't miss it for the world," Ethel replied between sips.

Rhoda was anxious to speed things up and get out of there. "Ladies, Sal told us that you could give us more information about the red van that side-swiped Sal yesterday. Is that true?"

Ethel and Vivian Merlot looked at each other and nodded. They obviously worked as a team. Vivian said, "You go first Ethel."

"Okay, let's see. There was a lot of writing on the side of the van. And a picture of a fish, a dolphin, and…"

"It wasn't a dolphin, honey. I told you it was a whale."

"It was not a whale Vivian. It was definitely a dolphin. It was jumping out of the pool, and it had a big smile on its face."

"No, you're wrong Ethel, it was a—"

Rhoda interrupted. "Ladies, the van had a pool on it?"

"Yes! A cartoon of a swimming pool." On this Ethel and Vivian both agreed. "It was right above the address," Ethel added.

Rhoda's eyes lit up.

"Oh! You saw the address?"

Ethel and Vivian looked at each other again. They frowned and shook their heads. No, they had not seen the address.

"But wait a minute," Vivian added, "It did say Deerfield Beach."

"You sure honey?" Ethel asked.

"I'm positive."

Rhoda looked at Phil. Now they were starting to get somewhere. A red van with a picture of a pool and a smiling fish of some sort that was from Deerfield Beach. What kind of business would that be? An aquarium store? A fish market? Rhoda shook her head. Those kinds of businesses wouldn't have a swimming pool on their van. Rhoda stared across Sal's backyard at the gently circulating water in his crystal-clear pool. Suddenly, she got it!

"Thank you, ladies. You've been a big help."

"We have?"

"Oh yes. Come on, Phil. Let's go."

"Please stop by again, Rhoda. Maybe you and I can spend an evening around the old piano singing a few tunes from *Dear World*. It's a most underrated musical, you know." Sal started leading them back to the house but Rhoda, afraid Sal would spot Wallie's misdeed on the living room carpet, asked if they could exit through the garden.

"Oh. Of course. Right this way."

Phil and Rhoda waved to Sal and the Merlots as they headed down the walkway. "So, what are you thinking Rhoda? I saw that light bulb go off in your head. You couldn't wait to get out of there."

"Phil, we are looking for a pool maintenance company that's based in Deerfield Beach."

"We are?"

"Yup." Just then Rhoda's phone rang. "Hold on Phil. I have to take this." Rhoda gripped Phil's arm as she answered the phone. She didn't want him to drive off just yet. "Hello?"

"Rhoda, it's Leila. Good news. I'm on an American Airlines flight taking off in a few minutes. I land in Fort Lauderdale at four. Can we meet at Momo's at six?"

"Absolutely. I'll see you then." Rhoda hung up and looked at Phil. "Phil, can you meet us at Molly's at six? We're gonna see if we can find Molly's cell phone."

"Uh, sure Rhoda. But you said "us." Who's coming? Dolly? Or Sage?"

Rhoda rolled her eyes. "I'll explain later. Just be there at six, Phil. Come on Wallie. Mommy's got work to do!"

Chapter Twenty-One

Goodwin's Morning

FOIE gras, foie gras, foie gras…

The 600-thread-count Matouk ivory bedsheet that arrived from Neiman Marcus only four days earlier lay rumpled in a ball at the foot of the bed. Two of the three king size pillows were on the floor, the other propped like a defeated boxer against the grey suede headboard. The matching fitted sheet still bore the damp imprint of the bed's recent occupant. Goodwin's night had not been an easy one. Standing on the balcony of his 24th-floor apartment watching a lone runner sprint across the deserted shoreline, he sipped a tasteless cup of black coffee and struggled to remember details from the ugly dream that woke him violently from an intermittent sleep at 5am.

He was traveling with his parents in a moving car, but no one was driving. Only eight or nine years old, maybe ten, his slender frame was wedged between his mother and father in the back seat. Intense sunlight filled the front window, making it impossible to see where they were going. His mother was screaming, yelling something about foie gras. The car was traveling fast, speeding, possibly airborne. Outside there were hundreds and hundreds of chickens squawking, pecking at the windows, fighting to get in. His mother let out a long electrifying scream as the car hurled up, up into space and—

Goodwin shut his eyes, bringing an end to the disturbing images. He inhaled the salty ocean air and felt his throat tighten. A cough quickly turned into a gag. Turning away from the unobstructed ocean view, he found his sorry reflection staring back at him in the UV tinted glass. He looked like a bum. He was a bum. He lifted his arm and sniffed. He stank like a bum. He slid open the balcony door and walked through the arctic living room air to the kitchen, glancing sideways at the five kilos of coke stacked monumentally on the imitation Noguchi coffee table that had recently set him back two thousand dollars. As he poured the remnants of the tepid coffee down the drain, he remembered the weekend trip that had triggered the frightful dream.

The three Goodwins, father, mother, and little Nate, had driven to his Uncle Tony and Aunt Claire's chicken farm on the outskirts of Eldersburg, Maryland. Young Goodwin had never met his father's brother or his wife but always looked forward to the fancy Christmas card they sent each year along with an opulent red and gold foil wrapped gift basket filled with ginger cookies shaped like reindeer, orange marmalade in a crystal etched jar, smelly cheeses wrapped in porous beige cloth, and cold meats with funny names like Soppressata and Mortadella. Nate's mother, Irene Goodwin, did not envy their relatives' wealth—Irene and Ken Goodwin were quite comfortable themselves—but she detested the "showy" lifestyle that they unabashedly put on display every chance they had; the enormous house with the circular driveway, the top-of-the-line Mercedes, the imported Limoges dinnerware purchased during a first-class trip to France. Their efficient and pristine 350-acre farm was one the major suppliers of chicken to the Perdue company. Shiny gold plaques on the walls of Uncle Tony's office were a testament to their success: the 1992 Award of Distinction presented by the Perdue Company to Goodwin Farms; the 1993 Award of Merit presented by the Perdue Company to Goodwin Farms; and an enlarged photo of Frank Perdue shaking Uncle Tony's hand, in a sterling silver Tiffany frame, all hung over an Italianate rose marble mantel with a vase of brilliant white peonies pointing up at them. "They're a bunch of snobs," his mother disdainfully tossed over her shoulder from the front seat of their 1995 Chevy Caprice Classic as they drove back to Glen Burnie. Unknown to Irene Goodwin, her son did not share her criticism. In fact, young Nathaniel felt quite the opposite. He was infatuated with the heavy engraved silver soup spoons, the lavender scented bath soaps, and the state-of-the-art McIntosh stereo system. All the way back to Glen Burnie, he vowed that one day he too would buy such wonderful things and eat only foie gras and meaty lobster tails coated in warm melted butter served on a silver platter.

Years later, when Goodwin attended Johns Hopkins and shared classrooms with students from affluent families, his boyhood infatuation became an all-consuming obsession. He studied fashion as seriously as he studied his medical textbooks. Battistoni dress shirts and Ferragamo loafers lined his dorm room closet. To mark the occasion of his first professional position as a forensic pathologist, he purchased a Piaget watch on his modest Cuyahoga County salary, a purchase which did not go unnoticed by the other members of the staff.

Goodwin stared blankly across the kitchen island into the living room. The Piaget watch lay tauntingly next to the five kilos of coke on the thick glass tabletop. An awakening, so sudden and pure, slowly spread across his chest along his shoulders and down his bare, limp arms. His fingers tingled and his feet went numb. An overwhelming feeling of euphoria engulfed his entire being. He knew then, in an instant, unfailingly certain, that he was done. He was free. It was over. Today was the day he'd end it all. He kept his gaze fixed hard on the table as he headed to the bathroom.

A half hour later, showered and shaved, hair neatly combed and wearing a crisp white shirt, he drove down Federal Highway to begin what would become his final day as Broward County's Deputy Medical Examiner.

Chapter Twenty-Two

Slow Journey

JIMMY allowed himself just a second to catch his breath. The only thing escaping was time. Hopping inch by inch, he had finally made it to the side of the garage. Now all he had to do was saw through the rope and free his hands. He quickly discovered that it wasn't as easy as he had thought. His wrists were tied tightly, allowing only teeny-tiny up and down movements. It would take longer than he had expected it to, but he was sure, if he stayed at it, the razor-sharp table leg would eventually cut through. Up, down. Up, down. It was exhausting and painful work. He couldn't see his wrists behind him. Was he making progress?

On the other side of the door, the brothers started arguing again and one of them turned off the music. Silence. He stopped sawing and listened. A few seconds later the sound of an engine needing a tune up pulled in the driveway. A car door slammed. Breezy was back. Jimmy's heart started racing. The only thing he could do now was to return quickly, and hopefully quietly, to the spot where they had left him. He began hopping back.

He could hear Breezy's voice in the kitchen. A crash on the floor. Someone laughed. Then they all started talking over each other. Cabinet doors banged. The noise was a good thing. The loud conversation camouflaged the sounds the chair legs were making as they scraped across the cement. Someone started... loading a dishwasher? Good. He was halfway back to where he had started. Only two feet left to go. Then the unthinkable happened. One of the chair legs snagged in a crack on the garage floor. He was stuck. Jimmy hopped harder but he couldn't free it. He struggled trying desperately to propel the chair forward. It wouldn't budge. He took a deep breath, tightened his muscles, and summoned every bit of energy he had in him. He gave it...one...last...push... The chair tipped over. He landed on his left shoulder like a sack of potatoes dropped from a ladder. His neck stretched painfully toward the floor. He bit down on his lower lip to keep from moaning. The voices in the house suddenly stopped. They had heard the noise. Jimmy lay there, waiting. He couldn't see the door or the two steps. He held his breath. The door opened. The overhead light snapped on. Footsteps on the stairs. Then footsteps walking toward him. Closer and closer. Breezy's dirty pair of brown Rockport's stopped six inches from his face. They were so close Jimmy could see the frayed laces. He closed his eyes bracing for a kick.

"Well, what have we here?" Breezy punctuated the remark with a sinister chuckle. "Have you been a bad boy?"

Jimmy looked up from his position on the floor. He expected the worst.

"Stand him up fellas."

They jolted him upright but miraculously didn't notice the chair had moved. Jimmy could not believe his good luck; however minimal it was. Breezy held out a half-eaten Kit Kat bar. For the first time Jimmy noticed Breezy's hand. It was missing a finger. How had he missed that? Eyes locked on Breezy's hand, he shook his head.

"Eat it." Breezy shoved the candy into Jimmy's mouth.

It tasted chalky, like a spoonful of dry plaster. He swallowed painfully. Breezy walked over to the metal worktable and leaned against it. "Okay. Here's what we're gonna do. The four of us are gonna take a ride to your friend's house."

"Rhoda's?" Jimmy asked.

"NO NOT RHODA'S!" Breezy had had enough of Jimmy mentioning Rhoda's name. "Not her, fuckface." He glanced over to Ignacio and Martin. "Although maybe we should pay her a visit, boys. Put that fucking dog of hers through a meat grinder to teach her to mind her own fucking business. But we won't. Not yet." He started walking to Jimmy's chair. "We're going back to your *other* friend's house. Dearly departed Big Molly." With his three fingered handed he started stroking Jimmy's matted hair. "Now, if you're telling me the truth, and you don't have her cell phone, I'll give you a chance to prove it by finding it at her house. Once you do, and hand it over, maybe we'll let you go home. How's that?"

Jimmy nodded his head. Maybe he could escape when they brought him to Molly's. He would run down the block and yell and scream. He'd…

Breezy snapped his fingers. Ignacio rolled up the garage door. The sudden shock of afternoon sun was blinding. Martin ran outside to the red van and backed it up into the garage, stopping inches from Jimmy's feet. Ignacio opened the van doors and together the brothers untied Jimmy from the chair, hoisted him up, and threw in the back of the van. He landed painfully on his left shoulder, the same shoulder he landed on when the chair fell over. This time he let out an audible moan hoping someone would hear. The door slammed shut. The van lurched forward and stopped. He heard the garage door roll down.

"I'll meet you there, fellas." Breezy popped a gummy bear in his mouth and watched the van drive off. He tossed Jimmy's red bandana on the grass, got in his car and followed them to Wilton Manors.

Chapter Twenty-Three

Fishing

RHODA opened her laptop and typed "pool maintenance Deerfield Beach" in the Google search bar. She wasn't surprised when a list of twelve companies came up. After all, it was Florida. "Just start at the top," she said to herself. She clicked on the first company, Aquabliss. Their well-designed website was quite colorful but didn't have an image of a dolphin or a whale happily jumping out of a pool. Next! Aqua Buddy Pools. While there were no smiling fish to be found anywhere on Aqua Buddy's web pages, they did have a photo of an annoyingly happy little girl popping out of the water. Rhoda quickly closed the browser. The image had reminded her of that snarky Myrtle.

Rhoda continued clicking down the list looking for anything similar to what the matchy-matchy Merlot ladies had described. Nothing. Not one fish. Three of the companies didn't even have a website. Rhoda's gut told her those were the companies she should be focusing on. A company that only had an address and a phone number might be the type of company that was on the shady side, flew under the radar, a company that would hit people on their heads and throw them in the back of vans. She nodded to herself and decided she'd pay each one of the three a visit. She took out a notepad and wrote down each address. Of the three, Pool Service Ninjas sounded the most dubious, so she'd start with them. They were five miles north on Powerline Road. She checked the time. It was a little past two. Leila and Phil were meeting her at six at Molly's, so she'd have to hurry. "Come on, Wallie. We gotta hustle."

Wallie whined at the mention of his name and looked lovingly at Rhoda through sleepy puppy eyes. He was peacefully curled up in his soft, fluffy pale blue calming bed with his favorite toy, a pink squeaky unicorn. He didn't seem interested in going anywhere. Rhoda contemplated letting him stay home when her phone rang. She looked at the caller ID. "Well, well, if it isn't Camille of the Manor," Rhoda said to herself when she saw Robin Kradles' name. For the pleasure of calling Robin "on the carpet," she'd gladly delay her departure a few minutes. "Robin! Darling! I have been so worried about you! How are you feeling? Much better I hope?"

"Oh yes Rhoda! Back to normal. It's a miracle!"

"It certainly is!"

Rhoda's sarcasm went unnoticed. "It was just a twenty-four-hour bug."

"What was his name?"

"Excuse me?"

"I said I hear it's going around. You should take yourself on a little holiday, Key West perhaps. Didn't you win a free night at Island House? I seem to recall that."

Robin didn't respond.

"Robin? Are you there? I said didn't you win a free night at Island House?"

"Uh, yes, I did. But I can't seem to remember where I put the voucher… I'm such a scatterbrain sometimes… c'est la vie, as they say… Anyway, Rhoda, the reason I called was to thank you for hosting for me at Spencer's last night while I was laid up in bed. I'm sure it was a wonderful evening!"

Rhoda gritted her teeth and narrowed her eyes. Scatterbrain my ass. Robin Kradles was one of the most organized people Rhoda knew. So organized, in fact, that she filed her CVS coupons first alphabetically then by expiration date. Rhoda was not letting her get away with it. No, sir. "Excuse me, dear? I didn't quite hear you. Did you say, 'legs up in bed'?" Fucking, were you?"

"Rhoda! Really! I was sick as a dog…"

Rhoda had her prey cornered. She went at Robin full throttle. "More like on your knees in the doggy position, you cunt!"

"Whhhaaaat?" Robin sheepishly replied.

Blood rushed to Rhoda's cheeks. An angry torrent of profanity spewed into her iPhone so rapidly that poor Wallie snuck out of his soft, fluffy bed and hid behind the trashcan under Rhoda's desk. "OH NO YOU DON'T! You tired old lying bitch! Did you think I wouldn't find out that you were screwing around in the hot tub at Island House while I was doing YOUR job!! YOUR FUCKING JOB! Why didn't you tell me you were going to Key West? I still would have covered for you! Don't you know me by now?"

The wrath was followed by a long silence. Rhoda knew the drill. She started counting to ten. When she got to nine, the sweetest, most melodic dulcet tones reminiscent of Cinderella's Fairy Godmother filled Rhoda's ear.

"I love you, Rhoda."

"I love you too, honey." This was how all their fights ended. A ten-second screaming match followed by professing mutual love. "Look Robin, I gotta run. I have a few things to do, and I was out the door when you called."

"Sure honey. But really, thank you for hosting Drag Bingo for me. Let me know if I can return the favor."

Rhoda stopped mid-goodbye. Yes, there *was* something Robin could do. Something that had been gnawing at her ever since she visited Sarge at To The Moon. It was those ugly Christmas tree ornaments. They just didn't seem right. "Actually Robin, I do need a favor."

"Anything darling. Go ahead. You know I'm here for you."

"Can you run over to To The Moon and buy a Christmas ornament for me?"

"Of course, darling! Which one?"

"On the left, when you walk in, hanging up against the wall, there are a bunch of hideous tree ornaments. They're cheap looking and the colors are funky, they're just not attractive. You have to look hard for them. They're not hanging in a prominent place. But trust me, once you spot them, you'll know it. They are butt uggggg-lee! Buy me one of those. Any one. I don't care which one. Oh, and don't tell Sarge it's for me. Okay?"

"Rhoda dear, I know you don't have any taste but why would you want one of those ornaments when they sell such lovely mermaids and glittery balls and stars…"

The bitch was back. Not have any taste? How dare she!

"Look honey, don't ask questions. Just get me one of them. I'll explain another time. And remember, don't tell Sarge it's for me, got it?"

"Got it. I'll get there this afternoon. I'm craving a tuna melt at Myth Gastrobar anyway, and it's right next door."

"Girl, that tuna melt is gonna go straight to your hips. You're already approaching plus size."

"Cunt."

"Bitch." Rhoda hung up and threw the phone in her bag, laughing at the insanity of her relationship with Robin Kradles. "Wallie! Where are you?"

Wallie poked his head out from behind the trashcan making sure the maelstrom had subsided. Rhoda jingled her house keys. "Come on sweetie! We're going to Deerfield Beach!" And out the door they flew.

Chapter Twenty-Four

Vat's for Lunch Dahlink?

ROBIN Kradles slinked along Wilton Drive wearing a tan London Fog trench coat with the collar turned up, large black sunglasses and a fabulous black silk Chanel scarf that dramatically encased her entire head. She felt like Diana Rigg in an episode of *The Avengers*, although any passing stranger would say the resemblance was minimal at best. The scarf, however, was one of her most treasured possessions. She'd paid full retail, $525.00, at the Chanel store in Aventura. She only took it out of the box on special occasions, today's performance meriting one of them. To complete the mod Brit-espionage look, she wore shiny black patent leather go-go boots with a modest two-inch heel. Practical but chic. Rhoda had given her a top-secret mission to carry out and she was determined to follow her orders to the letter and not mess anything up. Disguised as a cold war spy, she would quietly slither into To The Moon and buy one of those ugly Christmas ornaments that Rhoda explained were hanging from the ceiling against the wall on the left—or was it the right?—without letting Sarge know that it was her underneath the Chanel scarf and gigantic dark glasses and that she was buying the ornament for Rhoda Rage. Maybe she would feign a Russian accent, although on second thought she remembered she wasn't very good at accents, they all came out sounding a bit like Vivien Leigh in *A Streetcar Named Desire.* No matter. Feeling confident she was operating incognito, Robin hummed the *Mission Impossible* theme song as she hugged the storefronts, making her way to To The Moon. But first she'd pop into the Myth Gastrobar for a tuna melt on sourdough.

"Robin Kradles! Great to see you honey! Table for one?"

Fuck. Two minutes into her top-secret mission and already recognized, and by that hunky Sergio of all people, her favorite waiter at the Myth Gastrobar. Maybe it would help if she changed her lipstick color… She decided to try the accent. She dug into her memory banks and channeled the Natasha character from the *Rocky and Bullwinkle* cartoon series. "Vat? Robin? Who dat? I Natasha. Please yes. Table for von."

Sergio might have been the hottest waiter at the Myth Gastrobar but he was definitely not the smartest. He stared dumbly at "Natasha," blinking his eyes several times as Robin looked around deciding where to sit. He was confused by the strange accent and weird outfit but thought she might be having a bad day. His full plump lips flashed her a big toothy smile that showed off his recent investment in Invisalign. He liked Robin. She was a decent customer and she always ordered the same thing. "Tuna melt on sourdough and an unsweetened iced tea?" he asked.

"Vhy, how did you know darlink? I hear the tuna melt is very good here."

"Because that's what you always or—" Sergio stopped himself. Robin clearly didn't want anyone to know it was her. He happily decided to play along. "Coming right up, madam."

Jose and Fred, also on duty, and Al, the cook, were huddled together in the kitchen doorway when Sergio walked over to put the order in. "What's with Robin? She on drugs or something?" Jose asked. "She looks like Ingrid Bergman in *Casablanca.*"

"With that five o'clock shadow she looks more like Humphrey Bogart," Al chimed in.

"I think she's trying out a new character for her act," Sergio explained as he filled a tall glass with unsweetened iced tea.

Fred rolled his eyes. "I hope so. I don't know how many more times I can watch her Cher impersonation. She's a bit old for that don't you think?"

Everyone nodded in agreement.

"Honey, when you're too old to do a Cher impersonation, it's time to hang up your lashes," Al added.

Everyone laughed.

"Vat? Vat's funny darlinks? Tell me. Natasha vants to laugh too."

After the tuna melt and unsweetened iced tea, Robin, aka Natasha, applied a fresh coat of her brand-new Anastasia of Beverly Hills lipstick, in the shade Rum Punch, and paid her check in cash. She didn't want to use her debit card in case the staff at the Myth Gastrobar were suspicious it might be her. She was pretty confident her disguise was successful. She thought Sergio might have recognized her at first, but when he kept calling her "madam" she was convinced he didn't know it was her. Plus, she left him a five-dollar tip, just in case, to keep him quiet.

"Goodbye darlinks. It vas fabulous."

Fred, Jose, and Al stood stone-faced at the counter watching Robin exit. Sergio was already picking up the five-dollar tip at the table, excited Robin had been so generous. She usually left a buck. "Bye Natasha! Come back again when you're in town."

"Oh, I vill darlinks. I vill." Maybe it was the excitement of her covert mission or the mayonnaise in the tuna melt, but the minute Robin stepped out the door she knew something was wrong. Her stomach rumbled and she felt a loosening in her bowels. She turned around and ran back inside.

"Did you forget something Natasha?" Fred asked.

"No, darlinks. I just need to use the little girl's room."

Sergio, still playing along, gave directions. "It's that way."

Robin rushed across the dining room to the two unisex bathrooms in the back. Both doors were locked. She rattled the handles.

"Be right out," came a voice from behind door number one.

Robin started jumping up and down thinking it would help take her mind off the urge. It didn't. She squeezed her ass cheeks together and started praying. "Hail Mary full of grace. The lord is with thee." Suddenly the urge passed. "Huh. False alarm." Feeling much better, she calmly walked back through the dining room and waved goodbye to Sergio, Fred, Jose, and Al who, all stood perplexed by the counter.

Once outside, she took a deep breath and looked up at the bright afternoon sun. Natasha was going to give Sarge a spectacular performance. Still humming the *Mission Impossible* theme song, she walked three doors down to the entrance of To the Moon, placed her hand on the door handle, pulled her shoulders back, and readied herself. But before she stepped inside, she was interrupted by someone rudely shouting at her from across the street.

"Hold up!! Wait!"

Robin turned and lowered her dark glasses. Ugh. Ashanti.

"Robin? Is that you? Hold up. I want to talk to you. Fucking traffic. I can't cross. Wait."

Ashanti darted across Wilton Drive narrowly avoiding a cyclist who gave her the middle finger as he passed. When she reached To The Moon, Robin grabbed her elbow and dragged her halfway down the block.

"Ouch Robin! You got some strong grip."

"Ashanti, I can't talk right now. I'm on a very important mission."

"A mission? Sounds important."

Robin rolled her eyes. "I just said it was."

"What's the mission?" Ashanti asked.

"I can't say. All I can say is that's it's something important and that someone we both know has asked me to do it."

"Oh, you mean Rhoda." Ashanti was like a broken piece of Tupperware. You couldn't put a lid on it. Robin squeezed Ashanti's arm even tighter and clenched her teeth.

"I'll let you know tomorrow, darling. When I've completed my mission."

Robin started walking back to To The Moon as Ashanti stepped backwards off the curb still gabbing relentlessly.

"Tomorrow? Okay, Robin, I'll see you tomorrow."

Robin turned to give Ashanti one last exasperated wave. "WATCH OUT!" she screamed.

A red van sped down Wilton Drive, missing Ashanti by a few tiny inches. Ashanti trembled in the street, unable to move. Robin and two passersby rushed over to her.

"Oh my god. Are you alright?" Robin asked, pulling Ashanti back on the sidewalk.

"I'm fine, I'm fine," Ashanti replied, catching her breath.

One of the two passersby said, "That was the same van that knocked over Salvatore D'Angelo yesterday! Who the hell is that jerk?"

Ashanti's eyes widened. "It was?"

"Yes, it was. I remember it exactly. It had a fish painted on it and a swimming pool."

Although she didn't know how or why, Ashanti realized this was more than just a coincidence and that somehow it had something to do with Big Molly's demise and probably Robin's secret mission too. She knew she had to get the information to Rhoda. Suddenly it was Ashanti that wanted to get away from Robin.

"Robin, I gotta run. There's something I just remembered I had to do. See you later." And with that, Ashanti darted back across Wilton Drive, but this time she looked both ways before she crossed, and disappeared into Java Boys to call

Rhoda Rage and let her know about the reappearance of the mysterious red van.

Robin, back in her Natasha character, thanked the passersby profusely for their help, "Sank you, sank you, darlinks," and resumed the task that Rhoda Rage had instructed her to do.

Sarge was on his cell phone when Robin walked in. It must have been quite an important call because he didn't look up when she opened the door and the little bell went "ding." Robin, glad he was distracted, quickly headed to one side of the store. She looked up at the ceiling. Now where were those dreadful ornaments? Keeping her back to Sarge, she walked the perimeter of the store, searching, searching, until, at last! She spotted them! God, they were ugly. The offensive baubles were hung too high for anyone to reach them without assistance. She looked around to see if there was a step stool that she could use. She spotted a blue plastic milk crate that held an assortment of stuffed animals. The milk crate seemed, at first glance, sturdy enough to support her 162-ish pounds. Robin poked her head around the corner of the aisle. Sarge was still engrossed in his phone call and hadn't even noticed that he was no longer alone in the store. Good. Robin smiled at how easy this seemed to be going. She suddenly had a flash that she wouldn't even pay for the ornament. Why should she? It was so ugly. Rhoda hadn't said anything about reimbursing her and she was already out four extra dollars for the tip she left Sergio. With Sarge on the phone and unaware of her presence, she would stand on the milk crate, take down an ornament, slip it into her coat pocket, and nonchalantly walk out of the store. She tip-toed back to the milk crate and quietly turned it over, dumping the stuffed animals on the floor. She turned the milk crate on its side and slid it under the ornaments. This would definitely work. Unfortunately, due to Robin's excitement, or the mayonnaise in the tuna melt, the moment she stepped up on the wobbly milk crate, the rumbling in her bowels returned. She had to use a bathroom, and fast. Robin felt a trickle of sweat run down the side of her face. There was no time. She had to act quickly and get out of the store. She clenched her ass cheeks together to keep it in, reached high up for one of the ornaments, and… the left heel of her go-go boot locked in one of the holes of the milk crate.

"Motherfucker," she mumbled to herself. She jiggled her foot trying to free the heel but it was stuck solid. To steady herself, she held on to the wire rack directly in front of her that contained dozens of *That Girl*, *I Love Lucy*, and *Gilligan's Island* eyeglass cases. The ornaments were only two inches above her head, hanging from a sturdy metal bar. She decided to grab one while she was up there and worry about her heel later. She reached toward the closest ornament, a faded red one. The milk crate then started to bend unsteadily in the middle and sway from side to side. Robin stopped moving and, holding on to the wire rack in front of her with both hands, tried to steady the crate. The good news was that the urge to use the bathroom had once again passed. When the crate stopped swaying, she reached up and pulled at the faded red ornament. It wouldn't budge. The ornament was so tightly anchored to the metal bar by a twisted wire that you'd need a box cutter or razor blade to free it. She tried another, an ugly green one. Same thing. She wondered why Sarge had made them so impossible to detach. Yes, they were ugly but didn't he want to sell them? She reached all the way to her right, as far as she could, to try the silver one with half the glitter missing, when, with one hand on the ornament and the other still holding the wire shelf, she lost her balance and went flying backwards into the opposite shelf, which displayed *Betty Boop* red wine goblets and *Miley Cyrus* shot glasses. Everything came crashing down! The two shelves caved inward, scattering the eyeglass cases, the wine goblets, and the shot glasses all over the fluffy stuffed animals that she had dumped on the floor. Robin landed right between an orange orangutan and a polka-dot pony with big black glass eyes that were staring right at her. A *Miley Cyrus* shot glass was wedged in her lower back. Broken glass covered everything. She tried getting up but an excruciating pain shot through her left ankle.

"Ohhhhhh," she moaned. The silver ornament she had grabbed hold of as she fell had come down with her and had broken into thousands of tiny pieces. She felt something sharp prick the index finger of her right hand. Her finger was starting to bleed. Then she noticed something else. Her hand was covered in a sparkling white crystalline powder. It looked just like cocaine. Was it? Robin licked the side of her hand. It sure was. Good stuff too. The taste brought Robin back to her disco days in Cherry Grove on Fire Island. It was the summer of '91. She was thirty-three years younger and lived on the dance floor. Ah, the good old days. Robin yanked off her crooked sunglasses and looked around at the mess; shot glasses, eyeglass cases, greeting cards, stuffed animals, and broken wine glasses lay scattered about dusted in snowy white powder like a winter morning's first snowfall. Her eyes widened at the realization that the cocaine had been hidden inside the silver Christmas ornament. Robin looked up at the ceiling and ran her eyes across the dozens of other ugly ornaments, the red ones, the green ones, the gold ones, the blue ones. She started counting them. One, two, three… How much cocaine was up there?

"What the hell are you doing?"

Standing before her was a face that she hadn't seen in a long, long time and one she could never forget. "Well, well, well. If it isn't John Breezy," she sneered. She glared with contempt as Stretch Breezy stared back at her. "Or is it Stretch? That's what your lowlife friends used to call you, right, Stretch?" Robin said the name as if eggs were rotting in her mouth. "I always wondered what happened to you. Where a scumbag like you ended up. Well, whadda ya know. Right here in my own backyard. Wilton Manors. Last I heard you were passing bad checks in Pensacola. That right, Stretccccccccccch??"

Robin, head resting on a cocaine covered sheep, looked like Mae West reclining on a chaise lounge waiting for Cary Grant to arrive. She repeated Breezy's name over and over, rolling every letter off her tongue, mocking him.

"Stretcccccccccccch.   Haha.   Stretcccccccccccch Breeeezzzzy."

Breezy, his right cheek twitching at the taunts, suddenly recognized the voice of Richard Bailey, the brother of his ex-wife, Donna. "Richard Bailey! Look at you layin' there. You were pathetic then and you're pathetic now. Ha! What's with the get-up? Halloween is long over."

"Fuck you, Breezy." Robin leaned on her left elbow into the orangutan's gut, trying to raise herself up, but the pain from the fall and her twisted ankle was too great. She slumped back down on the broken glass, the eyeglass cases, and all the soft fluffy animals, fuming at the sight of a man she never expected to see again in her entire life. John "Stretch" Breezy. Goddamnit. She wouldn't let him get the best of her. She'd maintain the upper hand even from her lowered position.

She saw Sarge peeking over Breezy's shoulder wringing his hands and looking worried. Very worried. He signaled to Robin with his eyes, warning her not to challenge him. Breezy was dangerous and he didn't want to see anything bad happen to her. But Robin didn't care. After a twenty-year career doing drag in Wilton Manors, she had skin as tough as a Gucci handbag. "No, motherfucker. You don't get to ask the questions. Not after you walked out on my sister fifteen years ago, cleaned out her bank account—which, by the way, was her share of our parents' inheritance, her *only* savings—and on top of that, you stole our father's solid gold vintage Omega watch from her fucking dresser drawer!" Remembering the watch made Robin glance at Breezy's wrist. Sure enough, he still had it on. She could see the lovely mother-of-pearl face poking out from under his trench coat. "You goddamn pig turd. You give me that fucking watch before I rip your fucking arm off."

The site of the watch triggered a fury so great that Robin, forgetting the excruciating pain in her neck, back, and ankle, shot up like an arrow and lunged forward, her razor-sharp fingernails pointed directly at Breezy's face. Breezy quickly pulled a six-inch stiletto from his trench coat pocket and began slashing the air spastically in Robin's direction.

"Run, Robin, run!" Sarge yelled. "The back door!!"

The sight of the shiny tapered blade made Robin think twice about trying anything funny. She heeded Sarge's warning and limped as fast as she could on her twisted ankle to the back of the store. Only, Sarge wasn't giving her any helpful advice. He was warning her that Ignacio and Martin had just come through the back entrance. Robin, realizing this too late, fell right into Martin's waiting arms.

"Grab her, boys. Put her in the van."

Martin shoved Robin into the glaring afternoon sunlight as Ignacio opened the back of the van. Together they hoisted her delicate 162-ish pound figure and threw her inside.

"This bitch is heavy."

"Watch it, busters," Robin said, in response to the rough treatment at the hands of Breezy's thugs. "You're hurting me. Didn't your mothers teach you how to treat a lady?"

"Robin?" A low voice, barely a whisper, called her name from somewhere deep inside the van. She squinted and made out the shape of a person lying on the van floor. Whoever it was, they had been bound hand and foot. Robin didn't respond. The voice came again. Softer even. "Robin, get in and keep quiet. Come over here. In the back."

It was Jimmy! Robin, pulling her bruised and aching body forward, crawled along the van floor, heading toward her friend just as Martin grabbed her busted ankle. She felt a rope wrap around her skin. Then her arms were violently tugged back to meet her feet. The rope painfully twisted around her wrists and ankles. A final cinch cut deep into her skin.

"Jimmy, thank God it's you," she mumbled just as the van door slammed shut.

Chapter Twenty-Five

Lost then Found

RHODA dug her nails into the steering wheel of her car and let out a sigh of frustration waiting for a frail octogenarian to cross the street. With one tiny step at a time, the old woman struggled with her busted walker across SW 1st Court in Deerfield Beach. Wallie, thinking he was helping, started barking at her, which only caused the woman to stop directly in front of Rhoda's car, smile, and wave at the cute dog. Rhoda smiled back and nodded, rubbing Wallie under the chin. "Be nice Wallie. One day that'll be me."

The neighborhood the GPS had delivered them to was a derelict hodgepodge of run-down homes, abandoned properties, and vacant lots full of trash. Rhoda double-checked the pad of paper she had scribbled the address on thinking she had typed it in incorrectly. Nope. This was the block. It was the last address on her list and she wasn't too hopeful. So far, her search for a pool maintenance company that used a red van with a fish and a swimming pool on it had proven fruitless. Certain that she was wasting her time, she'd quickly drive by and then race down to Wilton Manors to meet Leila and Phil. If traffic was good, she'd arrive just in time for their six o'clock appointment.

Slowing her car to a crawl, she squinted out the car windows looking left and right for the house numbers. She passed 195. 189. The next three had no numbers. 175. 171. Then she saw it, half-hidden behind a dead Mazari palm, 167. Except for an unlit lamp perched between half-closed curtains in the front window, the drab, mustard yellow house looked vacant. This had definitely been a waste of time. Rhoda decided to triple-check the address by pulling the company up on her iPhone. She must have written it down incorrectly. The other places were at least businesses. The cell phone service was practically non-existent. If she held her phone over the dashboard, she had one bar. As she waited, she glanced in the rear-view mirror. A dark blue car had turned the corner and slowly approached Rhoda's Subaru. Rhoda held her breath, keeping her eyes locked on the car reflected in the mirror as it moved closer and closer and closer and—it passed by. The driver, a young man wearing a backward baseball cap was leaning forward, squinting, as Rhoda had done sixty seconds earlier at the house numbers. At the corner, he stopped, jumped out holding a plastic bag and two sodas in a cardboard drink tray and ran up to the front door where a young lady was already extending her arm for, what Rhoda assumed, was a Door Dash lunch. As the car drove off, Rhoda looked back at her phone, which confirmed that she was indeed in the right place. Deerfield Beach Pool Maintenance and Repair, 167 SW 1st Court. Rhoda thought about ringing the bell or peeking between the curtains but decided her time would be better spent looking for Molly's cell phone with Phil and Leila. She pulled into the driveway to turn around. Putting the car in reverse, she checked the side mirror to make sure she didn't further damage the already dented mailbox which was leaning precariously into the driveway. A spot of red on the dry grass next to the mailbox caught her attention. There was nothing about it that looked recognizable; it could have been a bottle or a bag, but it seemed to be recently placed, or rather thrown there. Rhoda put the car in park and got out. She bent down and studied the balled up pieced of fabric. Not wanting to dirty her hands or worse, catch an incurable skin disease, Rhoda gave the red cloth a tiny kick with her foot. When nothing crawled out from under it, she bent down, gingerly picked it up with the tips of two fingers, and gave it a shake. The fabric unfurled. Rhoda turned it around and there, printed in white block letters on the right-hand corner were the words *Cherry Grove, Fire Island*. She immediately recognized it. It was Jimmy's red bandana! She looked at the house. Could this be the place? She decided it was a good idea to peek through the window after all. She threw the bandana on the front seat, but before she could close the car door, Wallie went wild. He sniffed the cloth frantically then began shaking it furiously in his mouth from side to side further confirming in Rhoda's mind the bandana was Jimmy's.

"Good boy Wallie. Wait here." But Wallie had no interest in being left behind. He dropped the bandana and jumped out of the car before Rhoda closed the door. He ran up the driveway and started sniffing crazily under the garage door. As Rhoda approached, he began scratching wildly along the bottom in a desperate attempt to get inside. Rhoda banged hard on the garage door and yelled "JIMMY!" There was no response. She reached down, grabbed the handle with both hands, and with all her strength rolled it open. Wallie bolted ahead. He started running around a metal folding chair that stood directly in the middle of the garage. Then he put his nose to the ground sniffing along the cement floor all the way to the two steps leading up to the kitchen door. Rhoda hesitantly approached the door. With one foot on the lower step, she waited a few seconds listening for sounds. When none came, she quietly twisted the door handle and softly pushed the door open praying it wouldn't squeak. The house was dark. She picked up Wallie, stroking the top of his head to quiet his whimpering, and entered the house. "Hello? Anyone home?"

She moved a few feet into the kitchen. There was a pungent odor of garlic and rancid oil coming from several greasy take-out containers hastily shoved into an open trash can. Rhoda tiptoed into the dining room, noticing the coffee cups and half-eaten bagels on plates. Before moving farther, she looked over her shoulder to make sure she was still alone. She remembered she had left the car running and debated whether to go back and turn it off or keep moving through the house. If she left now she knew she'd be too scared to return so she kept going, down the hall, past a bathroom, a closet crammed with pillows and blankets. She opened another door.

"Ahhhhhhhhhhhh!" An ironing board fell out hitting Wallie squarely in the snout. His little heart began racing in his chest. He struggled desperately to free himself from Rhoda's motherly grip but Rhoda only squeezed him tighter. There was one room left at the end of the hall and she was determined to see inside, with Wallie for protection of course. She walked slowly, carefully, all senses on high alert. She peeked inside. "Oh." Her mouth hung open. A folding table was set up in the middle of the room. Keeping her arms locked around Wallie, she gave the door a push with her foot and saw a second table had been set up on the other side of the room. There was something on the tables. Many things. The objects were arranged in orderly rows running the length of the tabletops. She had seen these objects before. They were the same ugly Christmas tree ornaments that Sarge had on display at To The Moon. Only here, the tops of each ornament were removed and alongside them lay aluminum funnels and other devices that could be used to fill them. But with what? What had she stumbled into?

There was a crash in the hallway behind her. With no time to study the ornaments and funnels laid out across the tables, Rhoda turned and bolted. The ironing board had shifted and fallen across the hallway, causing the sound and blocking Rhoda's exit. Rhoda shoved the ironing board to the floor almost dropping Wallie whose rear legs kicked and squirmed against her waist. She raced through the kitchen and down the two steps leading into the garage. Leaving the garage door wide open she jumped in her running Subaru and sped down the block on her way to Wilton Manors.

Chapter Twenty-Six

The Good in Goodwin

"I'D like to speak to Officer McConnell please."

"He's not in today. Is this urgent?"

"It's… No." Goodwin had procrastinated calling Phil all day, only to find out he wasn't in. He pushed his phone aside and began fidgeting with the silver letter opener he kept on his office desk. The letter opener, a gift from his parents upon graduating Johns Hopkins, was engraved with his initials, NHG, the H standing for Harrison, his paternal great-grandfather. Harrison Lowell Goodwin was a formidable man in his day, and was considered one of the most preeminent Baltimore judges of the early 1900s. So distinguished and respected, in fact, that his name was inscribed along with twenty-three other jurists around the frieze of the Supreme Bench Courtroom in the Clarence M. Mitchell, Jr. Courthouse in Baltimore. Goodwin recalled the day his father took him to the Courthouse and pointed to his ancestor's name.

"Remember Nate. Always keep your nose clean and do the right thing. Your great granddad is watching."

And he had. Up until now. He picked up his cell and put it back down.

"Everything okay?"

Goodwin smiled at Kate in the doorway and nodded.

"I brought you a cruller. It's from that bakery on Las Olas. You've been so quiet all day. I thought some sugar might help."

"Thanks, Kate."

Kate lingered to see if Goodwin felt like talking. "I'll be transmitting last month's stats to central. Let me know if you have anything to add or amend."

"Will do." Goodwin pointed at the cruller and gave Kate the thumbs up.

Kate's eyebrows knit and an undisguised look of concern crossed her face. "I'm fine, Kate. And thanks for the cruller. My favorite." She felt something was wrong, she knew her boss pretty well, but decided pressing the matter would only push him away. She'd wait until he was ready to talk.

Vacantly, he steered the cruller around the desk with the letter opener, thinking about what he would say to Phil when they finally spoke. He hadn't eaten anything since he walked in six hours earlier. The euphoria he felt in the car driving to work had faded by the time he pulled into the parking lot. He kept himself busy every minute to avoid thinking about the five kilos of coke sitting on his living room coffee table. When everyone had gone to lunch, he had stayed behind and worked straight through on an autopsy of a young man killed in a three-car crash on I95 in the middle of the night. The kid was obviously racing, lost control of the car, flipped over the divider, and slammed head-on into a truck. Not a pleasant way to go, but quick.

He took a small bite of the cruller. The sugary sweetness ignited his appetite and brought back memories of Maryland summer mornings when school was out and there was nothing to do but go fishing with his dad. He tore off larger and larger pieces of the cruller, eating voraciously until it was gone. The sugar had done its work. He picked up his phone and searched for Phil's cell number. It rang three times before O'Connell answered, a noticeable sound of surprise in his voice.

"Hey Nate. What's up?"

"You busy?"

"Am I busy? That's a loaded question. What a day. I was supposed to be off but, well. What can I say? I got my boy's bedroom painted. That was good."

"Oh."

"You called?"

"Oh yeah. Right. I was wondering if I can meet you somewhere. I need to talk."

"Sure. Everything okay?"

Goodwin hesitated a second before answering. "Yeah. Yeah. Where can I meet you?"

When Phil didn't answer right away, Goodwin thought he was changing his mind.

"Phil, you there?"

"Yeah. Just thinking about where to meet. How about meeting me at Molly's? On NE 23rd."

Goodwin's heart stopped.

"Why Molly's?"

"I'm meeting Rhoda there at six. Shouldn't take long. We can grab a beer at Myth. You know, the old Courtyard Cafe. After the day I had, I need to sit down with a nice, cold brew."

Goodwin considered this. He didn't want to see Rhoda or have her hear anything that he had to say to Phil. What he had to say had to be said one on one, privately.

"Nate?"

"I'm here."

"Good. Thought I lost you there for a second."

"Okay. I'll meet you at Myth. I'll be waiting inside."

"See ya there, buddy. Gotta clean these brushes before they're ruined. Bye."

Goodwin, still holding the letter opener—do the right thing, Nate—hung up and with lips moving, silently began rehearsing the speech he'd deliver to Phil over a beer at Myth Gastrobar. "Phil, I've gotten myself involved in a pretty, no make that very, dangerous…and illegal…matter. And I want to confess."

Chapter Twenty-Seven

Showdown

SLUMPED against his car, Phil McConnell opened his mouth wide and let out a big yawn. Stretching both arms high over his head, the six o'clock sun warming his face, he smiled thinking about how great his boy's bedroom looked after the paint job. With his new BOSE noise cancelling headphones planted firmly on his ears, he turned up the music on his cell phone and returned to reading the story about Lionel Messi's recent arrival in South Florida. Surprisingly, after painting a 12-by-15-foot bedroom, ceiling, four walls and trim, then cleaning out the brushes, putting the ladder back in the garage and two side-trips to meet Rhoda, he was still fifteen minutes early arriving at Big Molly's house. Not a very relaxing day but, hey, he did it. His wife Tracy, worried about where the boys would sleep after they had pulled all the furniture out of the room at the crack of dawn, insisted that he finish the job "no matter what" when he returned home from Sal D'Angelo's pristine shrine to Jerry Herman. Now, exhausted and achy, and still wearing the same blue paint-splattered shirt that was now even more splattered, he looked forward to a quick meeting with Rhoda, then a quick beer with Goodwin, and returning home to lots of praise from his kids and a good home cooked meal from Tracy. Dreaming of Heineken and lamb chops and drumming his fingers against his car to the sound of Greta Van Fleet, his favorite rock band, he was oblivious to the world around him and certainly did not hear the constant *bang-bang-bang* of Robin Kradles' broken two-inch heel against the inside of the red van that was parked only ten feet away.

Inside the house, a frantic search was underway for Molly's missing cell phone. Ignacio turned over the furniture, Martin ripped up the carpets, and Breezy emptied bookshelves and dumped out every drawer. Jimmy, at Breezy's gunpoint command, halfheartedly joined the search while constantly worrying about Robin hog-tied and gagged in the back of the airless van. Slowly and quietly, he steered himself toward the kitchen thinking he could slip out the back door, but an unexpected clock on the head from Breezy's gun butt quickly squashed that idea.

"Stay where I can see you. No funny business. You hear me?"

Jimmy moved to the dining table and started turning over the same four placemats again and again trying to look busy. He glanced out the window wondering if Robin had passed out from the intense heat. He winced thinking about the agony she must be in. Martin had stuffed her magnificent black silk Chanel scarf in her mouth and used the belt from her London Fog trench coat to hold it in place. Then he bound her wrists to her ankles using an old frayed electrical cord leaving her in a painful position on the hard steel van floor. Needless to say, she was not pleased. Her last words to Martin before the Chanel scarf went in were "goddamn shit-face motherfucker." Jimmy was wondering how long a person could live roasting in the back of an airless van when he noticed Officer Phil leaning against his car. He quickly moved away from the window to avoid bringing Breezy's attention to Phil's presence, which he took as an extraordinary turn of events. He wasn't sure why Phil was outside Molly's house, or why he wasn't wearing his uniform, nor did he care. It could only mean one thing, impending freedom for him and Robin. Phil's presence thirty feet away was the best piece of luck he'd had since Martin and Ignacio threw him in the van the day before in Rhoda's parking lot. Maybe it wasn't Phil? He took a step back and snuck a quick second look to make sure his eyes weren't deceiving him when he saw an Uber pull up in front of the house.

"Hey. Get away from that window. Keep working."

Jimmy jumped and turned back to the table, lifting the *People* magazines and putting them back down, moving them around and dropping them to the floor. When he bent down to pick them up, he saw Leila Engermann heading up the walkway to the front door. Another miracle! Leila! He'd be free in no time. But how could he warn her that Breezy had a gun?

"Excuse me. Are you looking for someone?"

Leila, hand on the doorknob, turned at the sound of Phil's voice. "Who are you?"

"I'm a police officer. And you are?"

Leila looked Phil over, the shorts, the headphones. He certainly didn't look like an officer. "Can I see some ID?"

"It's my day off. I'm waiting for someone." Phil suddenly remembered Rhoda saying another person would be meeting them at Molly's. "Oh! You must be Dolly. Or are you Sage?"

"What?"

"Rhoda said to meet her here at six and someone would be joining us."

Suddenly Rhoda's Subaru turned the corner, sped down the block, and came to a screeching halt behind the red van. Rhoda jumped out, tossing Wallie, whose enthusiasm from the fast car ride bordered on uncontrollable, in the backseat.

"Leila! Phil!" Rhoda ran around her car and stumbled, leaning against the van for support. It was then she noticed the color. "Holy shit! The van!"

Fierce banging came from inside. Leila and Phil ran to Rhoda who struggled for words.

"It's…it's…it's Jimmy. Jimmy's inside."

Phil grabbed the door and gave it a yank. The three of them fell backward onto the hood of Rhoda's car and stared at the site of Robin Kradles wiggling like an earthworm on the van floor.

"Robin!" Rhoda jumped in and started to untie her. She worked desperately at the knot on the belt tied around Robin's mouth. Once undone, she pulled out the scarf and gave it a shake. It was wet and full of teeth marks.

"Oh honey! What have they done to your Chanel!"

Robin, still bound hand and foot began to sob. "It's ruined!"

"Never mind that. What happened?"

"They got Jimmy. He's in the house. He's with that slime bucket John Breezy. And two others."

"John Breezy?"

"My sister's ex-husband. Rhoda, he's dealing drugs. Right here in our neighborhood."

"What?"

"John Breezy. He's a drug dealer."

Rhoda supported Robin's back while Leila worked on the knots binding her hands and feet. Phil moved closer to hear every word.

"You know those Christmas ornaments you wanted me to get? They're full of coke!"

"No!"

"Yes. I pulled one down and it broke. Coke all over the floor."

Phil made a start for the house. Robin panicked. "Careful Phil! He's got a gun!"

Just as she said this a shot came from the front window of Molly's house, shattering the glass.

Phil ducked and ran to his car as Rhoda, Leila, and Robin huddled for safety in the van. He opened the driver's side door and crawled in, unlocked his glove compartment, and removed his firearm. Then he called the station.

"Hello? It's Phil. I need backup. Shots fired at 525 North East 23rd Street. Hurry." Phil rolled over on the seat and jerked back at the sight of Nathaniel Goodwin leaning over him. Phil pointed his gun.

"Don't shoot. I can help."

Phil saw Goodwin was unarmed. "Go back to the van and tell them to stay down. We're waiting for backup."

"Got it."

Within seconds the sirens of two Fort Lauderdale Police cars could be heard quickly approaching the block. The officers jumped out, guns drawn, shielding themselves behind their cars. One of the officers, Janna Kelly, made her way to Phil. "What's happening?"

"There are four inside. One armed. One possible hostage. Only one shot fired." A second shot rang out from the house and hit the side of Phil's car. "Make that two."

Jose, Fred, Sergio, and Al ran out the back door of the Myth Gastrobar followed by several customers wanting to find out what was happening. Goodwin noticed them, and with arms waving wildly, jumped out from behind the van to warn them off.

"Get back inside! Now!"

A third shot was fired. The bullet struck Goodwin in the chest. He crumpled to the ground. Officer Kelly and Phil ran low to the pavement and dragged Goodwin's body behind the van. The bullet wound was serious and blood turned Goodwin's immaculate white shirt to deep scarlet in seconds. Officer Kelly got on her radio as Phil applied pressure to contain the bleeding.

"Man down. Send an ambulance."

Goodwin could barely whisper. "Phil. Phil."

"Hold tight. An ambulance is coming."

"There's no time. You need to hear this. My apartment. There's… there's…" He was drifting off.

"What? What is there?"

"Coke. Coffee table. It's Breezy's. I'm…I'm…sorry." Goodwin's head collapsed in Phil's arms, his eyes staring blankly up into the tire well of the van. He was gone. Phil looked at Officer Kelly then gently laid Goodwin's lifeless body on the pavement. Kneeling beside his dead colleague, Phil quickly unbuttoned his blue paint splattered shirt, took it off, bunched it up, and formed a soft pillow placing it tenderly underneath Goodwin's skull. He saw the other three officers spread out and run down the sides of Molly's house. In the back of the van, Rhoda cradled Robin who was still unhinged by the teeth marks she had left in her Chanel scarf.

"Do-do-do you-you-you think the-the-the dry cleaner can get them out?" she sobbed.

Rhoda, listening closely for more gunfire, gently stroked Robin's lopsided wig and pulled out a red Dunkin' Donuts coffee stirrer that was poking through the tangled hair.

"I don't know honey, I don't know."

Officer Tez Cedeno, covering the alley on the left side of the house, looked for a window or side door. His partner, Officer Jake Hoburg, and Kelly's partner, Officer Michael Wilk, moved down the right side of the building. As Cedeno slid along the house, his back to the wall, gun drawn, he heard a sound. Ignacio had run out the back door and was racing across the yard toward a neighbor's fence, ready to hop over.

"Freeze!"

Ignacio kept running. Cedeno bolted after him. Just as he was clearing the fence, Cedeno grabbed his ankle and pulled him back with such force, the chain link tore through his pants and cut deep into his right thigh.

"Don't shoot. Don't shoot me. Please."

Cedeno cuffed him and patted him down. Ignacio moaned in pain, blood soaking the backyard dirt. Cedeno turned and headed toward the back door. He whispered in his radio. "I'm going in."

The back door was wide open from Ignacio's exit. Cedeno moved into the kitchen without making a sound. He listened. The house was quiet. He crept slowly past the refrigerator, the sink, the pantry door, careful of each step, and slowly began his way down the hall, gun pointed up and poised at his left shoulder. He reached the archway to the dining room, pressed himself against the wall behind the arch where he couldn't be seen, then slowly peaked around. Breezy stood to the side of the shattered front window, searching the street, gun in hand, ready to take another shot. Shielded by the archway, Cedeno couldn't see anyone else in the room. It was a clear shot to Breezy and Cedeno knew he had to take the chance.

"Hands up."

Breezy turned and aimed, but Cedeno fired first and hit Breezy's shoulder. Breezy's gun fell to the floor. Cedeno dove into the room and kicked the firearm to the far side of the room then knocked Breezy to the floor. The sound of a siren filled the room. Cedeno pinned Breezy to the floor with his foot and scanned the perimeter of the room, gun still drawn. The front door slowly opened. He took aim. His partner, Officer Hoburg, carefully slipped inside. Cedeno held a finger to his lips and gestured with his head toward the bedroom to let Hoburg know where others might be hiding in the house.

Outside, the paramedics attended to Goodwin's body as Phil went to the back of the van to check on Rhoda, Leila, and Robin. Rhoda extended a hand and pulled him in.

"Everyone here okay?"

Robin looked longingly at Phil's shirtless torso and whimpered "my scarf."

Rhoda nodded reassuringly. "Go on, Phil. We're fine."

Phil hopped out of the van and headed to Molly's front door while Officer Kelly signaled she was heading around the back. Inside, after cuffing Breezy to a leg of Molly's china cabinet, Cedeno and Hoburg moved back-to-back toward the bedroom and listened intently for Jimmy and Martin. Kelly tiptoed through the open back door into the kitchen. She moved toward the hall, passing the refrigerator, the sink. Her head turned at the faint sound of a click. She reached for the pantry door handle with one hand and pointed her gun with the other. She yanked the door. Squeezed against the shelves of kitchen utensils, spices, and cans were Martin and Jimmy. Martin's left hand covered Jimmy's mouth, the other hand pressed a grapefruit knife to his throat. Cedeno and Hoburg appeared in the kitchen doorway. Kelly held up a hand to stop them from moving further.

"Okay, put the knife down and step out. There's no need for this. Right? This is not how we want this to end is it?"

"Move out of the way. Let me walk out of here. If you don't, he gets it."

"Okay, look. I'm moving away. See. I've moved to the side."

Martin hesitated.

"Who's with you?"

"The other two officers. They're standing right over there to my left."

She called over her shoulder, keeping her eyes locked on Martin.

"Put your guns down, boys. I've got this. We're gonna let him walk out of here through the back and no one gets hurt."

Martin's eyes darted past Officer Kelly, trying to see the other two officers.

"Are you telling the truth? There are only two?"

"Only two. And me. I swear."

Kelly could see Officer Wilk and Phil through the kitchen window. She prayed that Martin believed her.

Martin slowly inched out of the closet; the serrated edge of the grapefruit knife held firmly against Jimmy's neck. Kelly slowly lowered her gun and moved back several steps to allow him access to the door. Martin backed towards the open door with Jimmy up against his chest. When he reached the opening, he shoved Jimmy deep into the kitchen and ran. Jimmy stumbled and fell, blocking Kelly's exit. Before Martin's foot hit the dirt, Phil sprang from the side and tackled him to the ground while Officer Wilk jumped over them, leaping inside.

"Everyone good in here?"

Kelly helped Jimmy to his feet while Cedeno and Hoburg ran back to the dining room to deal with Breezy.

"Yeah. We're fine. Go help Phil. I'll take care of this guy."

Calm befell the block. After a few minutes, Rhoda stepped out of the van and looked at the house. She signaled to Leila all was safe. She ran to her car to check on Wallie while Leila helped out Robin, whose ankle had swollen to triple its size stuffed in the shiny black boot. Like munchkins in *The Wizard of Oz* after Dorothy landed on the witch, Jose, Fred, Sergio, Al, and all the customers from Myth Gastrobar slowly started coming out the back door. Robin, never one to disappoint an audience, held up her black scarf and mouthed "my Chanel."

The paramedics waited to see if someone else needed attention before they left the scene. Wallie, who had hidden on the floor of the car as gunshots flew around them, jumped up on the dashboard as Rhoda approached. Through the windshield she could see he had Jimmy's red bandana in his mouth. Rhoda opened the car door just as Officer Kelly came out of the house helping Jimmy walk to the waiting paramedics. Wallie bolted past Rhoda and raced to his friend.

"Wallie! And my bandana!"

Rhoda, tears in her eyes, ran up and threw both arms around Jimmy's shoulders.

"Jimmy! I'm so glad you're okay. Now where's my wig, motherfucker?"

They both laughed as Robin hobbled up to join them, the Chanel scarf once again wrapped majestically around the now crooked wig, the broken sunglasses sitting askew on the tip of her nose. Leila headed toward the house. Rhoda remembered Molly's cell phone.

"Hold on Leila! I'm coming."

As they approached the open front door, Cedeno stepped out. Hoburg led Breezy down the walkway to the ambulance, his hands cuffed behind his back, his coat sleeve torn and bloody from the bullet graze to his shoulder, his face contorted with pain. Robin froze. Behind the dark glasses her eyes locked on the man who had ruined her sister's life. Forgetting her twisted ankle, her broken heel, her busted sunglasses, her crooked wig, and her ruined Chanel scarf, she threw her shoulders back and walked straight up to Breezy. "I believe you have something that belongs to my sister." She looked at Officer Hoburg and pointed to Breezy's wrist. "It was my father's, officer. This low-life scum stole it from my sister, his ex-wife, before he split town. I'd like to have it back if I may."

"With pleasure ma'am."

Hoburg roughly thrust Breezy's arm forward.

"Owwwwwwwwwwww."

Robin undid the clasp and slid the watch off. She noticed Breezy's missing finger. "I told you you should've thrown out that busted Weedwacker." She turned on her broken heel and limped down the walkway to Jimmy, waving the watch high in the air. "You haven't changed a bit, John Breezy. You're like school on Sundays. No class."

Chapter Twenty-Eight

One Robin Kradles Special Coming Up

LEILA picked up the broken picture frame that was wedged under the TV console and smiled as she remembered the night, many years ago, when the photo was taken. There was Molly, a younger if not thinner Molly, sitting on a stool at the outdoor bar at the Alibi. She had a cigarette in one hand and was raising a martini glass to the camera with the other. Rhoda, wearing a fabulous magenta beaded gown and Leila, in cutoff jeans and a Ramones T-shirt, stood on either side of her laughing and pointing at something to the right of the cameraman. "Do you remember the night we took this Rhoda?"

Rhoda tiptoed between the fallen books and broken knick-knacks strewn across the dining room floor. "Let me see."

Leila put her arm around Rhoda. She squeezed her waist tight as side by side they examined the details of the snapshot remembering the past.

"Yes, I do. That's my Ditzi Gainmore dress. It must have been ten years ago."

"More like twelve. I'm still wearing boys' clothes."

"And look at my Nokia! God, remember flip phones?"

"Momo had a rotary until a year ago. It was right over there next to the TV. The cord reached all the way to the kitchen!"

"I remember! Molly's house was one big booby trap."

They laughed as Rhoda slipped the photo in her bag. "Let me take it home and put it in a new frame. It'll be my little present to you. Take it back to Chicago and put it somewhere nice."

A warm silence was accompanied by a gentle tropical breeze blowing softly through the broken front window. It carried the aroma of gardenia and lemongrass. They looked at the debris, the ripped open throw pillows, the shattered glass, the end tables lying on their sides. The door of Molly's treasured china cabinet had been yanked so far back it now hung at a painful forty-five-degree angle toward the floor. Leila ran a hand through her hair and groaned. "What a fucking mess. And who, I wonder, will pay to clean it up?"

"Keep dreaming, Leila. When Lady Justice tips her scales the shit flies all over the floor."

Rhoda kicked around the papers that had spilled from Molly's overturned trash can.

"No cell phone here."

"Or anywhere. It was new, too. I gave it to her for her last birthday." Leila realized the finality of what she had just said. Her last birthday. Tears ran generously down her cheeks. Now it was Rhoda's turn to comfort Leila. She put her arm around her shoulders as Leila rubbed the back of her hand over her eyes.

"iPhone 15. Oh well."

Rhoda guided Leila over to Molly's chair, one of the few pieces of furniture standing upright.

"You two doing okay?" Officer Phil stood bare-chested in the archway of the dining room. He cradled an exhausted Wallie in his arms. Rhoda smiled when she saw Wallie was wearing Jimmy's red bandana tied loosely around his neck.

"Phil, put a shirt on. This isn't the Ramrod."

Phil blushed and handed the sweet terrier to Rhoda.

"Where's Jimmy, Phil?"

"I sent him home. Told him to come down to the station tomorrow and make a statement. Hopefully he gets some rest."

Rhoda lowered her head and stroked Wallie's back. "I'm sorry about that Goodwin fella."

"He wasn't so innocent, you know."

"What?"

"Just before he died, he told me there was coke, lots of it, back at his apartment. Breezy's coke. We've got some guys heading there now."

"*I knew it.* I knew he was involved in all this. And Sarge?"

"We'll see what happens. Officers Kelly and Wilk are over there now. Hey, you two have any luck with finding the cell phone?"

Leila shook her head. "We should give up looking. At least for tonight."

Phil headed for the door. He stopped and turned around. "Rhoda, you ever figure out what that note meant?"

Leila looked up from sorting through the papers strewn across the dining table top. "What note?"

"Oh, Leila. I guess I forgot to tell you. Jimmy slipped this strange note under my door the day Molly died. It seems to have been written by her." Rhoda dug around in her handbag. "Here." She handed the piece of paper to Leila, who slowly read the words out loud.

"THE GOLDFISH KNOW. Well, one thing for sure, it is Momo's handwriting."

Rhoda sighed and looked over at Phil. "I guess we'll never know what she was trying to tell me."

"Wait a minute."

Phil and Rhoda turned and watched Leila move to the open front door. Leila looked out on the street then glanced back down at the note. "I think you're wrong. Com'ere."

Leila stepped aside so Rhoda and Phil could get a clear view. They stared in silence at the red van parked in front of the house. On the side in bold white letters, it read DEERFIELD BEACH POOL MAINTENANCE AND REPAIR. Underneath, in a playful yellow font were the words THE GOLDFISH BROTHERS KNOW BEST! To the right, a cartoon of a happy goldfish jumped off a diving board into an aqua blue pool. CALL TODAY!

QUACK QUACK QUACK

Wallie's ears shot up.

"What was that?"

QUACK QUACK QUACK

"It's Momo's cell phone!"

Leila looked at her watch. It was 7pm, time for Molly to take her evening pills.

QUACK QUACK QUACK

Rhoda's head turned left to right looking for the source. Phil moved into the dining room toward the sound.

"Where's it coming from?"

QUACK QUACK QUACK

Leila pointed to Molly's chair.

"From over there."

Rhoda ran to Molly's chair and started digging her hand along the crevice between the seat cushion and arm. She slid her hand in deeper and deeper, running it up and down the sides of the cushion. "Voila!" Rhoda's hand flew high over her head holding up Molly's iPhone 15. She turned it on. "It needs a password! Leila, do you know it?"

"050395. Molly insisted I use my birthday when I set up her phone."

Rhoda typed the numbers. A picture of Leila popped up behind several icons.

Rhoda looked blankly at Phil and Leila. "What are we looking for?"

Phil ran over. "Check her photos." Rhoda tapped the icon. Phil and Leila huddled around Rhoda who squeezed Wallie under one arm as she scrolled through photo after photo of Breezy and his two henchmen carrying boxes through the back door of To The Moon from the red van. Rhoda, using two fingers, zoomed in on one of the photos. Ignacio was walking from the van towards the back of To The Moon carrying a box. Printed on the side of the box in big letters was one word, ornaments. Breezy was in the background holding the door for him. Rhoda handed the phone to Phil.

"Here Phil. Tell the DA it's an early Christmas present. Come on, Leila. You're staying with me. I could use a shower and a nice, cold Robin Kradles special."

"What's that?"

"The most refreshing beverage you ever tasted. It'll remind you of steamy nights in Key West, raffle prizes at Scandals Saloon, and Drag Bingo at Spencer's Corner."

"Raffle prizes and Drag Bingo?"

Rhoda laughed and headed out the door.

Chapter Twenty-Nine

Molly's Song

A familiar scent filled the midmorning air, greeting Rhoda as she stepped out of her car. Hand on the door, she stopped and looked around. She couldn't quite figure out what it was or where it was coming from. Even Wallie seemed to sense it, pointing his tiny snout toward the sky taking in quick short breaths. There were no flowers of any kind near the entrance to the church. It couldn't be perfume or cologne. She was parked too far away from the gathering group of friends standing outside Saint Mark's Episcopal waiting for Molly's memorial service to begin. And yet, the delightful fragrance was everywhere. It was a clean, fresh smell, like a load of laundry when it comes out of the washer, or the first whiff of a new bar of soap. Rhoda's mouth hung open. She spun around realizing what it was. Angel's Trumpet! But where? Where?

"Rhoda!"

Rhoda saw Ashanti heading toward her, in a pale blue dress that complimented her buxom physique. In her hair were six artfully placed rainbow barrettes. Wendy walked beside her and as they came closer Rhoda noticed they were holding hands.

"Molly got a good day for her memorial, right Rhoda?"

Rhoda looked up at the solid blue sky. "She most certainly did, Ashanti."

"You like my hair? Molly gave me the barrettes. Wendy put them in." Ashanti squeezed Wendy's hand and pulled her close.

Rhoda smiled. "They look lovely, Ashanti. Good job, Wendy."

They walked to the church entrance, stopping to say hello to Alfredo and Benny from Spencer's Corner who had just arrived together on Benny's Yamaha.

"Hello, Benny. Hello, Alfredo. You both look so handsome."

Benny adjusted his necktie underneath the leather jacket. "Oyé mami. I can't remember the last time I wore a tie. Is the knot okay?"

"The knot is fine. It's just a bit crooked. Here." Alfredo adjusted the tie then ran his hand through Benny's tousled hair.

Rhoda smiled at the budding relationship and rubbed Benny's shoulder.

"It looks wonderful, Benny. If Molly were here, she would have pinched your cute little Spanish cheeks."

Alfredo locked arms with Benny and leaned over to Rhoda. "I'm sure she would but which ones?"

"Rhoda, chica, I am so sad. Everyone misses Molly so much. I can't believe it's been two weeks."

"I know, I know Benny. But Leila said this was a day to celebrate, not a time for tears. You know Molly would not want to see us crying."

"I know mami, I know. But I can't help…"

Benny's voice cracked. The emotion of the day had even touched Alfredo, who turned his head so the little group could not see the teardrop running down his face.

"Let's go inside, boys, and find a place. It seems pretty full." Rhoda locked her arm around Benny's other elbow and together the three of them passed through the open doors of the church. Inside the stained-glass vestibule, Terry was handing out programs as Topher guided people to vacant pews. Terry, nervous as always, dropped the programs when she saw Rhoda walk in. Rhoda bent down to help pick them up noticing the little gold locket Terry wore around her neck containing a photo of her and Molly.

"Rhoda?"

"Yes, Terry?"

"We're taking up a collection to have a paver stone engraved in memory of Molly. You know, for the courtyard at the Pride Center. Would you like to contribute?"

"It would be my pleasure. Benny, would you hold Wallie?"

Rhoda opened her bag and pulled out a hundred-dollar bill. "Will this do?"

"Gosh. We're only asking people for five dollars. With this we can get a bigger stone."

"Good. Keep it. I owe Molly a lot more than this." As Rhoda took Wallie from Benny, she saw the lonely figure of Sarge sitting hunched in the last pew. He had been released on bail and was fully cooperating with the FBI's investigation of Breezy. From what Rhoda heard, albeit second hand from Ashanti, it seemed Sarge had gotten in a financial mess when his house in Dania Beach needed a new roof and his transmission died on his 2009 Audi all in the same month. Breezy came along and offered him a "no interest loan" with the proviso that Sarge allow Breezy to run his little cocaine operation out of To The Moon. Sarge knew it was wrong, but Breezy was someone you didn't easily say no to. Rhoda planned on being a character witness at Sarge's upcoming trial, as did Jimmy, Robin, and even Officer Phil. In fact, the whole of Wilton Manors was rallying behind him. Hopefully, together they could keep him out of jail and his magical emporium in business. Rhoda leaned into the pew. "Sarge. Sarge."

He turned and gave Rhoda a weak smile. She put her finger under her chin and raised her head up. He got the message and his smile grew bigger.

Topher tapped Rhoda's shoulder. "Father Grant is getting ready to start. Let's find your seat." Topher guided Rhoda down the center aisle to the spot he had saved for her in the front pew. "Don't forget. We're all invited to Rosie's for lunch. Leila reserved the entire patio. Molly stated in her will that she didn't care where the memorial service would be, only that we had to have a big party at Rosie's with an endless supply of—"

"I know. Fried pickles on each table. Molly loved those fried pickles."

Soft music filled the space. Rhoda recognized the tune but, once again, couldn't place it. She softly hummed along as she walked, nodding to Eli Tenner, the Mayor, and several Wilton Manors Commissioners. The place was packed. Everyone had turned out to remember Molly. Now, what the heck was that tune? Rhoda was certain she had heard it before. A flash of recognition. It was Sal's damn doorbell! "If He Walked Into My Life Today." She looked over to the side chapel, and there, seated regally at the shiny black Steinway, was Salvatore D'Angelo, eyes closed, head thrown back in a trance, swaying to the strains of the Jerry Herman melody. He wore a purple sequin three-piece suit, black patent leather shoes, and a silver bow tie. She felt a tug at her sleeve.

"Rhoda. Rhoda."

She looked down and saw Phil. He was sitting alongside his wife Tracy and their two twin boys, both wearing matching seersucker suits and brown penny loafers. One of the boys had made a paper airplane with the program and was desperate to fly it.

"We're coming to the lunch. Are you going?"

"I wouldn't miss it for the world. See you there."

Farther down the pew, Ethel and Vivian Merlot, in matching black satin jackets over snow white Polo shirts, sat holding hands as Gooch rested comfortably between them. Behind them was the gang from Myth Gastrobar: Jose, Fred, Sergio, and Al. Rhoda blew everyone a kiss and hurried to the front pew where a spot was waiting for her next to Robin Kradles who sat side by side with Sunny Conditions. When she slid in, Robin turned and gave her a peck on her cheek. Rhoda was thankful she was sitting next to Robin and not behind her, as Robin was wearing the biggest black hat ornamented with black marabou feathers and draped with thousands of white pearls. She looked like the Mad Hatter if the Mad Hatter did drag. Sunny Conditions, in a slightly smaller hat, a black silk fascinator topped with artificial cherry red roses, leaned over and gave Rhoda a wave.

"You both look fabulous," Rhoda whispered.

"Only the best for our Molly," Sunny replied.

Robin and Sunny turned toward each other and smiled.

"Friends at last," Rhoda thought.

"Will everyone please rise? Into thy hands, O merciful Savior, we commend thy servant, Molly McNamara. Receive her into the arms of thy mercy, into the blessed rest of everlasting peace, and into the glorious company of the saints in light. Amen."

As the congregation bowed their heads in respectful silence, Rhoda glimpsed Leila and Jimmy sitting together across the aisle. Both were holding note papers to help them remain focused when it was time for them to speak. Behind them was Molly's physician, Dr. Margarita Manfredini. Leila's request for a second autopsy was granted, most likely because Goodwin played a part in Breezy's operation, but the results were the same, myocardial infarction. Molly did die of a simple heart attack, after all.

"Please be seated for our first speaker, Ms. Leila Engermann."

After Leila, Jimmy spoke, recounting a funny story of how, during Hurricane Irene in 1999, Molly was forced to flee from the water rising mercilessly outside her front door and spend the night in the safety of Jimmy's second floor apartment. She had packed her overnight bag so quickly that she put on mismatched shoes, both left, and spent the next twenty-four hours switching them from foot to foot deciding which were more comfortable. After Jimmy, Father Grant concluded the service with a blessing over Molly's ashes as Salvatore D'Angelo returned to the piano to lead the entire assembly in a rousing rendition of Molly's favorite song, or so Salvatore D'Angelo claimed.

"The lyrics are on the back of the program. Let's bring it on home for our dear Molly. Here we go!"

One by one, voices joined in until everybody was singing. People stood, holding hands or arms around shoulders. Rocking, swaying to the music. Even Wallie and Gooch sang along, pointing their little snouts in the air and howling. The sound was deafening.

"The best of times is now!
And live and love as hard as you know how!
And make this moment last,
Because the best of times is now,
Is now, now!"

Rhoda cradled Wallie close to her heart and smiled. The intoxicating fragrance of Angel's Trumpet filled every corner, every nook of the cavernous church as the people of Wilton Manors held hands tightly and sang in joyful voice their loving goodbye to their friend, their neighbor, their stalwart queen, Big Molly McNamara.

Acknowledgements

Life, like a book, has many chapters. Each chapter filled with people, many are supportive and many are helpful. Some are just there when you need a friend. At 66, I'm unable to list every name of every person who helped me fill the pages of my life, but of the ones who have appeared in most of the chapters, well, I'd like to acknowledge them now.

First, and foremost, my husband, Kirk Bookman. Everything I have achieved in this life has been with his unwavering love, support and expert advice.

My sister, Elizabeth Baran. From Chapter 1 to today, she has been a true friend.

My nieces, Leah and Amanda. My extended family, Linda, Frank, Christina, Alisa, Ruwan, Redding and Hunter.

My buddy Eli, for keeping me young.

Richard Becker for letting me take Robin Kradles to the moon.

My editor, Michelle Levy. I could not have asked for a more supportive and on-board collaborator for this book.

My dear friends Cindy, Adrienne, Ronnie, June, Jim, and Joan.

My publisher, Amanda Lamkin. Thank you for seeing what I saw.

Our little joy, Wallie, four pounds of love. Without him, I'm certain this book would not have been written.

And last, the people of Wilton Manors for inspiring me as I ate my fish tacos at Rosie's or bought my holiday ornaments at To The Moon. It's a magical city and I'm happy to call it home.

Artist Credit

Lyrics included in this novel are:

Excerpt from "Indian Outlaw" by Tim McGraw

Excerpt from "The Best of Times" by Jerry Herman